'Are you afraid

'Of course not! I ha

'Anyone who excit
Vittorio finished for Lili.

'No, there is more to love than excitement.'

'But that is where it starts, *cara*. The pulsing of
the heart, the fire in the loins, that is where love
begins and that is what interests me about you.'

Dear Reader

With the long summer evenings, what better way to relax than by reading a selection of stories which really take you away from it all? With four exciting contemporary romances, Mills & Boon will transport you to some of the most exotic locations in the world. Enjoy the luxury of those places you always wanted to visit...surely the perfect chance to dream of your ideal man! Look out for our summer packs in your local shops or contact our Reader Service and indulge yourself in the world of romance!

The Editor

Natalie Fox was born and brought up in London and has a daughter, two sons and two grandchildren. Her husband, Ian, is a retired advertising executive, and they now live in a tiny Welsh village. Natalie is passionate about her three cats, two of them strays brought back from Spain where she lived for five years, and equally passionate about gardening and writing romance. Natalie says she took up writing because she absolutely *hates* going out to work!

Recent titles by the same author:

REVENGE
LOVE IN TORMENT
AN IMPERFECT AFFAIR
LOVE ON LOAN

A LOVE LIKE THAT

BY
NATALIE FOX

MILLS & BOON LIMITED
ETON HOUSE,   18-24 PARADISE ROAD
RICHMOND,   SURREY   TW9 1SR

First published in Great Britain 1993
by Mills & Boon Limited

© Natalie Fox 1993

Australian copyright 1993
Philippine copyright 1993
This edition 1993

ISBN 0 263 78077 5

Set in Times Roman 11 on 12 pt.
01-9307-50240 C

Made and printed in Great Britain

CHAPTER ONE

HE'S gorgeous, Lili mused, as they were preparing to land at Pisa airport. Beautiful eyes, the colour of ripe chestnuts, silky jet hair that fell endearingly over his kissable forehead, a wide, wide smile that had all the air hostesses hovering attentively near by. It was a pity about the missing two front teeth, but then you couldn't have everything.

'Who's meeting you at the airport, Carlo?' she asked the seven-year-old who had kept her so entertained throughout the flight from England. The child intrigued her. Travelling alone with just an airline aunty to keep an eye on him, he appeared to be a seasoned traveller, and that had saddened Lili. So young and already packed off to boarding-school in Surrey, and there was Lili believing the sanctity of family life meant something to the Italians. But she supposed little Carlo didn't come from a typical Tuscan family. He was travelling club class as she was—though her flight had been a last-minute self-indulgent splurge—he wore expensive clothes, his English was word perfect and the home he described in Tuscany sounded like *la dolce vita*. Lili recognised a touch of chic when she was confronted with it, even in the form of a small boy such as this.

'Papà will meet me,' Carlo enthused through that endearing gap in his teeth as the aircraft prepared

5

to land on shimmering hot Tarmac. 'Who will meet you?'

'No one,' Lili murmured with a smile, her thoughts more concerned with Papà than her lack of anyone warm and friendly to greet her in this warm and friendly country they were landing on. She bet Papà was quite a dish too if the good looks of his son were anything to go by. She brought herself to earth with a bump as did the aircraft. So was Mamma, no doubt!

'*Ciao*, Lili,' the boy said with a gappy smile and to her astonishment unclipped his seatbelt and stood up to give her a hug and a wet kiss on the side of her face. 'I think you are very pretty,' he added cheekily, and then he was gone.

She saw him once more, outside the airport, being handed over to his *mamma* by the airline aunty. His mother was beautiful, stunningly dark and sultry, Lili thought wistfully, though somewhat reticent with the son she probably hadn't seen since the beginning of the summer term. No hugs or kisses, but more an impatient hustle into the back of a glossy white Mercedes. For a second Lili's heart churned sadly. If Carlo were her son...

Lili blinked her hazel eyes against the glare of the hot sun and looked around for somewhere to hire a car. She was going to have to drive herself to the villa in the Tuscany hills in this searing heat, and that was her own fault for being so fiercely independent. Doubt creased her now. It hadn't been a very bright idea to refuse her late father's solicitor's very kind offer to meet her. Here she was in an alien country she had never visited before, armed only with a good sense of direction and a very tatty RAC map of Europe.

'Do you speak English?' she asked the young man in the car-rental cabin across from the airport.

'If I didn't I wouldn't get much business from you English,' he stated thornily.

'Point taken,' Lili breathed, delving in her jeans pocket for her credit card and driving licence. 'On behalf of the entire British race I apologise for our foreign language ineptitude; now can I hire a car for a few weeks without having to take a degree in Latin to get it?'

Lili eventually got her car, at a discount too for her cheek, and directions to the tiny village in the hills *and* an invitation to dinner when she brought the car back.

'Thanks, but no, thanks, *caro*,' she muttered to herself as she grated gears out of the airport on to the highway. 'I've taken a vow, you see: no more boring, dull men till I find one that truly excites me—and I mean *excites*.'

She occupied herself with that thought for a long time on the drive. Simeon had been her latest disaster. Dull, boring Simeon who had looked so promising on their first date but had turned out to be less interesting than an organic turnip on their second. Was she expecting too much of today's men? Was there such a thing as unquestionable passion, when your pulses leapt when *he* walked in the room, when your skin burned at the heat of his touch? Or was it all myth? A cruel myth that raised women's expectations only to drop them like a stone when faced with reality. Men were just dull—fact.

Lili smiled to herself as she headed up into the hills. If someone could read her mind they would think she was an empty-headed, romantic fool. There were more important things in life than a deep, meaningful relationship—weren't there? Of course, her career for starters. And once she was rid of this villa in the Tuscany hills she could afford to buy that studio in Fulham and then her career would really take off.

The smile turned to a frown. But how would she feel when she saw the villa her father had left her? She felt guilty for not coming here sooner. Hugo Mayer had been dead two years now and this was her first visit to the place where he had ended his days.

Funny how her father had settled here in Italy. Perhaps he'd sought inspiration from this hot, sweet-scented country, though inspiration hadn't been lacking in one of the world's most successful thriller writers. No, his mistress had brought him here and she was one of the reasons Lili hadn't come before. As a child she hadn't been allowed; as an adult she had been too afraid. Her father's leaving her the villa in his will had surprised her. Why hadn't he left it to the woman who had shared his life for so long? And where was she now? She certainly wasn't living at the villa; the solicitor had informed her it had been empty since his death.

At last Lili reached the tiny rustic village that was the last leg of her journey and twenty minutes later, after much arm-waving, scratching the name of her villa in the dirt with a stick and a lot of, 'Grazie, molto grazie,' she was riding the crest of a fearfully pitted dust track wondering if her father had lost his sanity in his later years. Of course, she didn't know what his sanity level was in those lost years as she hadn't seen him since she was twelve, but somehow she just couldn't imagine him living so far from civilisation.

'Heavens above!' Lili breathed at last as the plucky Fiat expired with exhaustion under a straw canopy that jutted out from the very simple stone-built Villa Libra. Shakily Lili got out, eased her clinging jeans from her thighs and stepped out into the sunshine to look up at the villa. It wasn't palatial, or even very pretty; in fact it was quite plain and not unlike most of the isolated farmhouses she had passed on the journey here. Lili wasn't exactly disappointed but she was quite mystified and not able to picture her father living here.

'So you are here at last. Let me help you.'

Lili spun round, so shocked that her hand went to her heart. A man had stepped out from the shadows of an olive tree and Lili's mouth parted in fear—or was it simple astonishment that someone so ravishing could step out of dusty nowhere and look so...so ravishing? He was tall and very dark-featured and had almost jet-black hair that she supposed was typical of the Italian race. And he was Italian, though his English was spoken with scarcely a trace of an accent, just that precision which was a give-away. He was elegant too, a surprise in this hot, dusty terrain. He wore a cool grey short-sleeved shirt and grey chinos, and though the clothes were smartly casual he screamed elegance. Bearing, that was it, and arrogance too. He looked *very* interesting.

'Oh, you startled me. I didn't expect anyone to be here.'

He said nothing but moved towards the car to haul out her holdall and the plastic bags of groceries she had bought in the village. She watched in astonishment as he carried them to the open door of the villa. She followed quickly, too hot and fazed to protest.

'Oh,' she murmured as she stopped on the polished flag-stoned floor of a very beautiful and tranquil sitting-room. She had expected a gathering of cobwebs and dust after two years but the place was sparkling.

Dumbstruck, she watched him place her bag on the sofa and stride assertively to the kitchen area of the vast room with her groceries. Confused, she blurted, 'Just a minute. I think there has been a mistake. I don't think this is the place...' It couldn't be. It was spotless and well cared for.

'No mistake,' he said coolly without looking at her. 'Unless of course you are *not* Lili Mayer.' He looked at her then and in spite of the distance between them his eyes had the effect of fast freezing her blood. They were oh, so black and penetrating, now rushing over her tall, slim form as if he were appraising a piece of sculpture to purchase for the odd corner of his home and not finding anything to his liking. She had the swift impression that the man was some sort of Italian aristocracy with his dark good looks and his brusque manner, which was quite ridiculous, for this part of the Tuscany countryside was definitely short of the likes of him.

'Yes, I'm Lili Mayer, but how did you know and could you please tell me what is going on?'

His dark eyes narrowed. 'Nothing is going on, Lili Mayer. I just wish to see you settled, though I must tell you you are not welcome here.'

His words froze her further but then she quickly recovered and stepped towards him because there was obviously a blunder being made here, though by whom she wasn't sure. 'Is this the Villa Libra?'

'It is,' he told her smoothly. 'The home of your father Hugo Mayer. Yes, you have the right place. You have made no mistake in getting here, but you have made a mistake by coming here.' He proceeded to unpack her groceries on to the marble work surface of the kitchen.

'Just a minute; you have me at a disadvantage,' she said brittly. 'You know who I am but I don't know who you are, and if anyone is making mistakes around here it's you!'

She snatched a packet of coffee from his hands, her fingers glancing off his in a very sharp, heart-stabbing contact that raised the hairs on the back of her arms. Yes, the man was very autocratic in bearing but not in manners. He looked at her as if he despised her and that was quite absurd because they had never met before.

'Who are you?' she breathed drily. 'And what right have you to be here in *my* villa?'

His eyes locked into the cool hazel of hers. 'I am Vittorio Rossi, and I have no right to be in *your* villa, but I have a right to air my objections to your being here and why, and I will do just that. I do not want this villa sold...'

'*You* do not want!' Lili exclaimed, heatedly wondering where he got his information from. '*You* have nothing to do with it! My father left me this property to do what I like with it and...'

'Your father left it to you to teach you something about the values of life——'

'Hang on——'

'I have hung on for two years waiting for you, Lili Mayer,' he interrupted coldly. 'And now that you are here I am not at all surprised by your attitude. Anyone who has not the common decency to attend her own father's funeral is not likely to have any warmth in her heart, any understanding of——'

Lili paled and her hand came up to clamp over her mouth. The tears were there before she could stop them and then the defence of her stinging emotions stirred to a blind anger as she interrupted wildly, 'How dare you? How dare you speak to me like that?' Oh, God, she was going to cry and she mustn't!

Coolly, calmly, he moved about the kitchen, opening cupboards and putting away the groceries. Lili was so shocked that she just watched him and fought the rawness in her throat. How could he have said that, and who on earth was he anyway?

Shakily she grazed her long tawny hair from her face. She couldn't have attended her father's funeral if she had wanted to, but *he* didn't know that and she wasn't about to explain to a rude stranger something so very personal. But it hurt to be accused of such a thing, something that had been out of her control, like most of her childhood. Her parents had divorced when she was a child, a messy divorce that had driven Hugo Mayer to France. The courts had allowed Lili as a child to visit him there but when he had moved to Italy with a mistress her mother, in a fury, had stopped the visits. Enter mistress, exit daughter.

'Would you like a drink?' he asked without turning to her. He poured two glasses of mineral water whether she wanted hers or not.

She shook her head, still recovering from his harshness. 'No, I don't want one!'

'You must drink in this heat.'

'Don't tell me what to do!'

'I insist!'

He turned to her then and fixed that insistence on her with the set of his jaw. Their eyes met and locked and there was something vaguely familiar about his, but hadn't she heard that all Italian men had dark, sultry eyes that could disrobe in a flash and make a woman feel her femininity? She took the mineral water he offered and dismissed the thought that he had mentally stripped her as being bizarre. He just didn't like her and resented her being here for some very peculiar reason.

'So how do you know so much about me?' she asked after drinking some of the refreshing water. She stood by the wide archway that divided the kitchen from the rest of the room. He was right about one thing—you did need to drink in this heat; her head was clearing, but he was so wrong if he believed she had never cared for her father.

He stood tall and strong in front of her, slightly intimidating but only slightly. She wasn't the nervous type normally but this was hardly a normal situation.

'I was a very close friend of your father.'

Lili's lashes flickered at that. 'You surprise me. From what I remember of my father he was always a very good judge of character,' she stabbed back.

For the first time he smiled, though it didn't go as far as those liquid eyes. 'He also had a sharp wit which his daughter has obviously inherited...' Lili slightly warmed to that dry compliment. 'But I suspect there is not much else you have taken from him.'

The warmth seeped out of Lili. Nervously she drank the last of her water and placed the glass down on the work surface without succumbing to the urge to slam it down.

'You have an attitude Signor Rossi, one that is most unpleasant——'

'Vittorio,' he corrected.

Lili shook her tawny head. 'I'm on Christian-name terms with people I like, Signor Rossi. *You* do not qualify.'

The second smile of the afternoon. 'As you wish, Signorina Mayer,' he said back, quite smoothly indicating that he thought the qualifications were mutual.

'So now the niceties of life are over with,' she gibed sarcastically, 'perhaps you would like to tell me why you feel the need to be so rude to me, or is that one characteristic of the Italians the outside world isn't too familiar with?'

'So how does the "outside world" view the average Italian male?' he asked, tempting her answer with a teasing glitter in his eyes.

Lili reflected that teasing glitter with some of her own. 'Usually believing there is more talent down-stairs than on the upper floor,' she tossed back at him wickedly and then held her breath in case she had gone too far.

This time the smile was one of genuine mirth. At least he had a sense of humour. Lili breathed with relief.

'Perhaps you see only what you want to,' he grinned, 'that we have only fire in our loins. But we do not pinch bottoms unless we think the bottom is willing to be pinched.'

For the life of her she couldn't imagine this man indulging in such a thing but his theory was amusing and interesting.

'Oh, yes, meaning they ask for it?'

'You say "they"—don't you mean "we"?'

Lili smiled at that. His command of the English language was perfect. 'I'm not that sort of girl,' she told him with good humour. She straightened her thin cotton print shirt over her jeans. 'Now I think the character analysis is over with, so would you kindly leave so that I can unpack?' She hoped he wouldn't prolong this conversation, because she was hot and tired and ached for a cooling shower.

He was still smiling as she turned away from him to pick up her holdall from the sofa.

'I cannot leave till I've explained.'

'Explained what—your earlier rudeness?' She swivelled back to face him and saw that the humour had gone from his eyes and mouth. It spurred her to lift her chin defiantly. 'Don't bother. This isn't an ongoing relationship, so you have no need.'

'I have no intention of offering you any explanations for my so-called rudeness, and as for this not being an ongoing relationship, that could be in the lap of the gods.'

His eyes were dark and moody as he delivered those disturbingly suggestive words and suddenly a great heat enfolded her and she wondered why. The Italian was awful—not in looks, they were beyond doubt good, but what lay beneath was a hard coldness she found disconcerting in spite of his flashes of humour.

'Mars, the bringer of war, no doubt,' she clipped, refusing to believe he might be flirting with her.

'Perhaps the Venus of Arles, the Roman Goddess of Love,' he suggested with deep mockery in his tone.

No flirt, this one, simply a teaser. She responded quickly and lethally. 'I've always thought that Roman mythology seemed very poor in comparison with Greek mythology. All those gods of earth and labour.'

His generous mouth tightened and he murmured, 'Meaning our priorities are practical rather than spiritual?'

She met his dark eyes and raised an impressed brow. 'You know your mythology.'

'And you, *cara*. I can see you have much of your father about you. We spent many enjoyable hours arguing our different beliefs.'

Somehow that hurt, knowing that this man had been so close to her father and probably knew more about him than she did.

'Well, I'm not my father and I can't say arguing with you is a bundle of fun, just very tiring. Now, you offered me some sort of explanation. If it wasn't for your rudeness, what was it for?'

He moved towards her and stopped, so very close to her that she could feel the heat of his body beneath his designer shirt. Like little Carlo on the flight, the man exuded Italian chic. She wondered what he was doing in this part of the world and she wondered why she was allowing his personal heat to invade her senses so.

'I need to explain how the villa works,' he told her softly.

Lili braved an incredulous smile. 'You make it sound like some piece of machinery. It's a house, not a car and I'm quite capable of finding out for myself how the plumbing works. Speaking of plumbing, I'm very hot and sticky and I'd like to take a shower, and I really don't need you here.'

'Ah, there you have brought me to the very point I wish to stress—the plumbing.'

There was mischief in his eyes and Lili's first thought was that there probably wasn't any plumbing! The house was isolated and far from that primitive village down the track...but surely not? Her father had been a wealthy man, not a Tuscan worker living frugally. There was plumbing; there had to be.

Vittorio Rossi seemed to penetrate her thoughts and know exactly what she was thinking.

'The values of life,' he murmured silkily. 'You will find out your father's intention soon enough. Come, I will show you.'

He went ahead of her, across the long sitting-room. Lili followed, quite numb with all that had happened so far. She still didn't know who this man was; she had a name, that was all, but she didn't know why he was here or where he had come from. And that remark about him not wanting the villa to be sold, delivered so deadly threateningly as if it was life and death to him—and where had he got that idea from anyway? She had only briefly hinted to her father's solicitor that there wasn't much point in keeping the place on . . . but, of course, he probably knew him anyway, being a friend of her father's.

She had no time to ponder over why the place was so spotless. It was well furnished with mellow antiques, books on shelves on the stone walls, a collection of porcelain on a mahogany table by the narrow window. There were homely sofas and chairs upholstered in rich dark tapestry and beautiful oriental rugs on the flag-stoned floors. As a textile designer Lili could appreciate the beauty of it all but she knew that the furnishings were the hand of a woman and the feeling was uncomfortable inside her.

Vittorio Rossi led her through this exquisite room to an inner hall with a stone staircase that led to the upper floor. He stopped at the foot of the steps.

'That is your father's study.' He nodded towards a closed wooden door. 'I hope you wish to peruse that in privacy.' He held her eyes as if searching for that wish.

'Of course I do,' she murmured quietly. 'In spite of what you think of me, I did love my father.'

He said nothing but led the way up the stone stairs and she followed softly behind him, wishing she could dispel this dragging feeling of guilt he made her feel. She hadn't had much of a relationship with her father and his death had left her with regrets which normally she could cope with; she really didn't need a stranger to challenge her so painfully.

The doors and windows on the upper floor were all open. A soft, warm breeze aired the atmosphere that she presumed must have been musty after two years of being closed up, but had it been closed? It didn't look as if it had and it didn't feel as if it had. It felt warm and yet airy and comfortable and sort of calm.

'My... my father lived...' Her voice faltered as Vittorio turned on the wide landing to face her as she spoke. She lowered her thick dark lashes. He had been a friend of her father's so therefore a friend of the... the woman he had lived with. He would know of her whereabouts.

'My father lived here with——'

'Emilia,' Vittorio Rossi told her, interrupting her as if to save her some sort of embarrassment. Lili was surprised and yet grateful for that small, helpful discretion.

So at last, after all these years of curiosity, she had a name, but somehow Lili couldn't say it. It jammed in her throat, quite painfully, even though she had convinced herself it didn't matter any more. Her mother had been bitter about... Emilia... but Lili held no hostility towards her, not then and not now. She was just saddened that her mother's bitterness had deprived her of her father for all those years and deprived her of a chance to meet the woman who had made her father so happy. And he had been happy. She hadn't known that before but she did now. Lili felt it; it was an atmosphere, an aura, here in this surprisingly simple house that had been furnished and lived in with love. That was what the Italian had hinted at—the values of life; they could be so very different when you were in love. Somehow she understood even though never having loved herself.

'Where is she?' she asked him bravely. She wanted to know; more than anything else in the world she wanted to know about her father's mistress. How must she have felt when she had found her lover had left his home to his only daughter, and why had her father done that?

It took a long while for her question to be answered, a long pause in which she had time to be aware of the scent of jasmine wafting in from an open window and the sound of cicadas buzzing outside.

'She is at rest, with your father,' Vittorio Rossi said at last, his voice oddly thick. 'She died three months after him, grief-stricken, not able to bear her life without him.'

Every sense in Lili's slight frame froze painfully. Her fingers coiled into her palms and her nails gouged at the soft flesh till she bit her lip with the self-inflicted pain. She physically felt the blood drain from her face till her head swam dizzily. A small, 'Oh,' was the most she could murmur through shocked white lips.

'A love like that...' was all the dark mysterious Vittorio Rossi said as he turned away from her and walked into one of the bedrooms.

Lili stood in the doorway, hesitant to follow him in, hardly able to think clearly. A great mountain of sadness weighed her down. She had never been in love herself, not properly, not a love like that... The thought of it made her feel queasy inside. It was beautiful and sad and tragic, and though she had never experienced it herself she could imagine how it felt.

She watched the Italian move towards the window, brush aside the fine lace and gaze out across the sweeping vineyards beyond the small balcony. The air was suddenly thick and heavy as if he too felt the great sadness. Lili wanted to break the silence but didn't know how. He saved her the trouble by suddenly turning to face her.

'I had one of my maids have this room made ready for you. It's the guest room. I hope it meets with your approval.'

He said it courteously, softly, not at all offensively, and she nodded her agreement, adding a feeble, 'Thank you,' followed by a forced 'But...but why...? I mean, how did you know I was coming? And...and the house, it's clean and well cared for.'

'I come every week,' he informed her quietly. 'I own the estate around here, the vineyards as far as you can see, the olive groves beyond. I was your father's nearest neighbour and his closest friend.' He waited for her to absorb that as if it was explanation enough and then added softly, 'Come here.' He raised his hand and beckoned to her.

Lili went to him, oddly relieved that he was nothing more sinister than a neighbour, but maybe there was more, though she couldn't imagine what. He had known her father very intimately, and his mistress, and seemed to presume a lot about her too; her curiosity was heatedly aroused.

She stood by his side at the window, close because she had no choice. She felt his heat again and her senses absorbed his own personal scent—a mixture of a sensuous cologne, the aroma of Italy, and just him.

'My home,' he informed her, nodding to the green beyond.

Lili wondered why she hadn't seen it before, but it probably wasn't visible from ground level. The villa in the hills was palatial, surrounded by huge lush maple trees. Though it was far away she assessed it as being huge and luxurious, a reflection of his own personality, grand and aristocratic and just a little imposing on the landscape! There were no other properties in view, just miles and miles of vineyards—his.

'It's very lovely,' she breathed.

'It means nothing,' he said abruptly and turned away. 'Come, I will show you the plumbing.'

With raised brows Lili followed him out of the room, wondering at that very strange remark of his and wondering about him and her father and Emilia, and, last but not least, there was a haunting worry about the plumbing too.

CHAPTER TWO

'WHY on earth should I do that?' Lili exclaimed, mild hysteria biting the back of her throat. What an oddity this man was. She was convinced he was enjoying putting her down this way.

'Because water is precious. I repeat, when you shower——'

'You don't have to repeat it, my hearing is perfect, but my comprehension is stretched to its limits. Are you telling me my father showered into a plastic bowl and kept the water to flush down the toilet?'

'Only when the water was running out.'

'When the water runs out?' she croaked idiotically. Oh, no, she might have to pump it up from a well.

'It is delivered by the tankerload——'

'You mean there is no running water here?' Lili gasped in astonishment.

'There is no electricity either,' Vittorio Rossi told her with a smooth smile that was obviously pure enjoyment.

'So...so how do I cook and how do I manage for light when the sun goes down?' she asked, wide-eyed.

'You cook by gas——'

'Well, that's something,' she cried with relief. 'Funny country, though—no electricity lines but gas on tap——'

23

'Bottled gas,' he informed her readily, his dark eyes dancing now.

Lili suppressed her anger. He really was enjoying all this. 'So when is it delivered?' she asked tightly.

'It isn't. You collect it from the village. The lorry stops in the Piazza Monday, Wednesday and Friday. The bottles are very heavy,' he added pointedly. 'I doubt that slight frame of yours will have the strength to lift them.'

'Oh, I'll find the strength, don't you worry about that,' she bit back. 'I've determination and grit, but if for some indeterminate reason they fail me I'll just imagine I'm going to heave them at your arrogant head!'

His eyes flickered uncertainly as if he realised he might have undermined her. 'It isn't a problem. I will bring them for you.'

The offer surprised her. 'And what about light?' she asked hesitantly.

'Oil lamps.'

'And when does the oil man cometh, the day of atonement?' She couldn't help her cynicism. None of this was what she had expected.

He smiled thinly. 'Your father would appreciate you.'

Lili tried to shrug that remark away but it wouldn't go. It wasn't for a stranger to comment on what her father might appreciate, but then who was the stranger? Desolately she turned out of the spacious bathroom they were standing in and stopped on the landing. 'How...how do I order water?'

'I have already done it for you. The tanker arrives in the morning; till then be sparing.'

Lili murmured her thanks, slightly chastened by his help. 'But how did you know I was coming?' she added.

'I know everything that goes on here.'

'Yes, I suppose you do,' she conceded, not wishing to argue that point. He appeared to own the whole area and the people along with it, no doubt. 'Is there anything more you want to show me?' She wanted him to go now because she was hot and tired and also because she wanted to be alone in her father's house.

'I see you are tired from your journey but there is something more I must show you.'

Can't it wait? she was tempted to ask, but she didn't want him back here, poking his very autocratic nose in where it wasn't wanted.

Once again she followed him like a lost lamb, down the stairs and through the kitchen to a laundry-room. No electricity, no washing machine, just a deep stone sink with a pounding-block to one side of it. Her father's mistress must have loved him deeply to suffer the hardships of hand-washing, unless they'd had a maid, of course, which was more like it.

Vittorio Rossi opened the door from the laundry-room and stepped out to a shadowy courtyard that took Lili's breath away. In that moment she began to understand her father's reason for being here.

A huge gnarled fig tree was its centre-piece; heavy with green fruit, it scented the air sweetly. The courtyard was cobbled and there was a high stone wall surrounding it. There were geraniums in profusion at its feet and bougainvillaea scaled its height, drooping scarlet, rust and cerise flowers thickly everywhere. There was thyme and rosemary growing in huge earthenware tubs and a vine in one corner with deep purple fruit hanging from the straw shades that swung from the top of the wall to the side of the stone house. Beneath the shades was a rustic table and chairs.

It was the table and chairs that claimed her full attention. 'My father would have worked here, wouldn't he?' she said softly, walking over to the table and running her fingers over the knotted wood.

'How did you know?'

Lili shrugged. 'Just a feeling, a sense of him still being here.'

'So you do have some warmth, some under-standing, some emotions.' His voice was softer.

Lili lifted her head to look at the man who had the power to hurt her so. 'Yes, I do. Why is that so surprising to you? He was my father and I cared.'

'You never came to him here.'

The cicadas filled the silence that lay heavily be-tween them. Lili lowered her lashes, not wanting to see his accusing eyes upon her. 'As a child I wasn't allowed; as an adult I was never invited,' she told him coolly and then she did look up to him and held his eyes steadily. 'I don't have any hang-ups about that but it seems to trouble you greatly. You accuse and suppose all sorts of things, Signor Rossi. You also claim to have known my father very well, so why do you suppose I was never invited?'

Lili noticed a small pulse throbbing at his jawline, powered by anger? she wondered. He probably didn't get very many women talking to him so bluntly. He said nothing because he knew nothing.

Lili spoke again. 'This courtyard, it's been well tended and, as I said before, the house has been kept beautifully; why?'

Slowly he came towards her, ducking to avoid the vines, then he was standing over her, adding more shadow to this secret corner of the courtyard.

'Because I knew you would eventually come, possibly baited by the thought of what you could make out of your father's estate,' he said coldly.

Lili's hackles rose but she controlled herself because to scream and yell at him would show he had got to her and she wouldn't give him that satisfaction.

'I get the very strong feeling that you are the one doing the baiting, Vittorio Rossi.'

He raised a dark brow and his eyes darkened further. 'You are very astute, Lili Mayer. Yes, I am spoiling for a row. Are you going to give me what I want?'

'If I knew exactly what you wanted I'd help you out of your crisis; you're obviously a very disturbed man.' As she said it she realised what she really meant was disturbing, not disturbed. She wished he wouldn't stand so very close.

'Perhaps I have good reason to be,' he said drily.

'Perhaps you'd like to tell me why.'

'Perhaps it's too early yet.'

'Too early?' she quizzed.

'Too early in this ongoing relationship.'

Lili smiled nervously. 'The relationship isn't going anywhere—now what was it you wanted to show me? Or is this it—this courtyard where my father worked? Am I supposed to be chastened by

it, influenced enough by sentimentality to not want
to sell after all?'

He gave her a cruel smile. 'I'd like to think that
it would be the reason for a change of your heart
but I doubt you have the capability of feeling
sentimentality.'

She held his cold eyes, terribly hurt by that, but
she was a past master at holding back hurt, though
there had been few people in her life to hold anything back from. Her mother had never been
around much and no father, no brothers or sisters,
only a few friends, no one particularly close.

He shrugged when she said nothing. 'It makes
no difference whatever you decide to do. The house
stays as it is, unsold.'

Lili didn't understand him but she recognised the
underlying threat. He had power, probably enough
power in this part of the world to stop it turning if
he wanted to. But he didn't frighten her, puzzled
her more than anything.

She looked deep into his eyes. 'Maybe by the time
I leave here you will wish you had never said that.'
She didn't mean it as a warning or a threat and
wondered what exactly she did mean by it; it was
just one of those gatherings of words that slipped
out from time to time.

'Maybe you will never leave,' he said throatily,
and in that instant Lili felt his power. Not the power
that could stop the world but the power to stop her
heart beating. Suddenly his hand came up and
touched her cheek. Like a butterfly wing, it grazed
her heated flesh till a small gasp of shock exploded
in her throat.

She tried to step back but there was nowhere to go. His fingers fluttered down her cheek and settled on her chin, holding her firmly in place as he lowered his mouth to hers. His lips were fire on inflammable silk, scorching her senses, tempting her weakness to breaking-point. What weakness? She had none, except at this delicious moment in time when she was melting in the heat of the day and the heat of the sweet pressure of his mouth. She tried to steel her heart against him, her lips against his, but something so odd was happening inside, something soft and silly, as if she had never been kissed before and this was the very first time.

Suddenly his arms were firmly around her, holding her hard against his body. She felt every strained muscle, every beat of his heart. She felt his need, his strength if she resisted, and she should be resisting, her dizzy thoughts told her. She should be slapping him down, because this was so bizarre, a stranger kissing her so intimately; but she couldn't move. His mouth parted hers and his tongue gently probed the soft, silky flesh of her inner lips. A tremor of deep desire flooded through her at the sensuous contact. She couldn't breathe, she couldn't think—nothing worked!

And then it was over and she stood gazing blindly up at him, struggling to form some words in the back of her throat. He said nothing but simply grazed the dewy moisture from her lips with his thumb and then raised it to his mouth and drew on it, his eyes hooded with desire as he watched her lips part with shock at the erotic movement.

Then her weakness was gone and Lili steeled herself against him, suddenly understanding what all this was about and despising him for it. Her hands came up but before she could push him away he moved back, dropping his hands to his sides. His face was as cold and unemotional as stone and she knew she was right.

'It won't make any difference,' she breathed hotly. 'A kiss won't alter my decision to sell.'

The corners of his mouth twisted cruelly. 'Perhaps it will take more than just a kiss, then.'

Lili shook her head in disbelief. 'You would do that, wouldn't you? Seduce me to stop me selling?' She smiled thinly. 'For that to work I would have to fall in love with you, and that's as likely as four feet of snow in this courtyard by nightfall.'

'You're a very determined lady, aren't you?'

Lili supposed she was. 'I know what I want; if that's determined, I am.'

'And does that go for affairs of the heart too?' There was mockery in his tone now as if the kiss hadn't put her down hard enough.

Lili's stomach tightened. She really didn't need this sort of conversation or his disturbing physical put-down. There were no affairs of the heart in her life, not that she wouldn't welcome one. She wanted to love and be loved but she'd never met a man to fill that need. This specimen in front of her certainly wasn't the one to lead her to Paradise where the earth moved on the hour, every hour!

'That's *my* affair!' she retorted. 'Now if you don't mind I'd like to unpack——'

'One more thing before I go. Come, I will show you.'

His abruptness and change of subject brought her to ground as if the kiss had never happened.

He crossed the courtyard and pushed aside the trailing bougainvillaea. For the first time Lili saw there was a wooden door behind it. She watched as he put his shoulder to it and it creaked open. It opened on to another small courtyard which was open to the vineyards beyond and sight of Vittorio Rossi's home high on the hillside. Lili followed him through the opening.

'Yes,' she sighed wearily. 'I've seen your Palace of Vesta and it's very nice——'

'The bell.'

'The bell?' she echoed stupidly, and then she saw it, behind her on the wall. A very old brass bell, ornate and tarnished with a length of knotted rope hanging from it.

'If you need me at any time,' he suggested, his dark eyes teasing her, 'I'll hear the bell.'

'It won't get any use,' Lili told him stoically.

'You will be alone here, pretty one, and most evenings the village men take their *passeggiata*, their evening stroll, through the vineyards. You are a curiosity here, you with your tawny hair and your beautiful body...' His eyes dragged over her once more and she felt the force of his power yet again.

'Are you saying I might be in some sort of danger?' she husked quickly to cover the alarm he had stirred inside her with those searching eyes of his. Strange, but the village men held no fear for her, but he...

'You could be a temptation. I have already succumbed,' he admitted, slowly and silkily.

'You have a motive for your desire, Signor Rossi. I doubt the village men have the same motivation.'

His eyes darkened broodily. 'A reason is not
always necessary. The heat of the night is sometimes enough.'

And the heat of the day powered through Lili at
the thought of what he was suggesting.

'I . . . I'm not afraid to be here alone. I'm quite
able to look after myself.'

'I'm sure you are,' he said quietly, 'Your waspish
tongue could halt the entire Roman army. But
nevertheless the bell is there if you need me, and I
mean that, loosely.' He added a small smile to go
with that and colour raced to Lili's cheeks.

'Thank you,' was all she said.

'I will come again tomorrow, when the water
tanker arrives; till then I wish you good day.' He
turned and went through the arched opening and
directly in to the vineyards to wend his way home
to his villa in the hills.

Lili watched him till the vines swallowed him up
and she could see him no more. What a strange,
strange, disturbing man.

She wondered about him the rest of the
afternoon, more so after inspecting the kitchen and
finding far more groceries than she had bought
herself. There were several bottles of wine in a stone
rack on one wall. Chianti, Lambrusco and
Sangiovese, all clean and not dusty as if they had
been left by her father. Vittorio must have brought
them, and not today, because he had no car with
him. There was fresh fruit—oranges, nectarines and
peaches—and a bunch of pink carnations in a vase
in the long sitting-room. Such thoughtfulness along
with his insults. Yes, a strange man.

Lili unpacked the few clothes she had brought with her—shorts and T-shirts and a couple of skirts and cool tops. She had planned on staying for about a month but now she wondered if that was possible. Rossi didn't want her here and he could prove to be difficult, but it really wasn't any of his business what she did with her father's house. None of his business whatsoever.

She awoke the next morning to the sound of car tyres on the gravel driveway. Surely not Vittorio Rossi so soon?

She jumped out of bed and quickly slid into shorts and a vest-top. The new day was as hot as the night that had preceded it but she had slept well enough. Barefoot, she padded downstairs.

'Oh,' she murmured, drawing her tousled hair back from her face as she confronted a stranger and not Vittorio Rossi's blatant arrogance.

The stranger in shorts and T-shirt smiled warmly. 'Stefano Bellini.'

Lili gaped and then realisation dawned. 'My father's solicitor. Oh, how kind of you to come...I didn't expect... Please come in.'

She had a full five seconds to take him in as he stepped past her into the long room. Youngish, fair-haired, tanned, sporty, not a typical Italian nor a typical solicitor.

They passed pleasantries about her trip over and then as Lili put a pan of water on for coffee, feeling slightly flustered by this unexpected early morning call, Stefano Bellini came to the point of his visit.

'I have a client who's interested in this property, very interested...'

Lili felt a shiver on the back of her neck as if someone were blowing on it to get her attention. She turned to the solicitor and smiled thinly because for some unaccountable reason she felt ill at ease in his company. Maybe it was the speed at which he got down to business that had her wary of him. There really wasn't a rush to sell.

'I know I hinted in my letter that I might consider selling but I haven't actually made up my mind yet.'

Last night in bed Lili had mulled over the idea. The sensible thing to do was to sell. She liked the place well enough but it would hardly get any use— possibly a couple of holidays a year if she could find the time, and she did want that studio. Rossi had disturbed her, but not enough to stop her selling if she wanted to.

'But this is a very good offer,' Stefano Bellini insisted, his pale eyes hardening. He reached in his briefcase for a sheaf of papers. Lili stared at them incredulously. Contracts? Surely not? Things moved at a tidy pace in such a sleepy area. 'I'm sure once you've seen these you'll want to jump at the offer.'

Lili took them from his outstretched hand. 'I'll give it some thought,' she told him crisply. She laid the papers down on the kitchen work surface and measured ground coffee into a jug.

'Aren't you going to read them?'

Slowly Lili turned back to him, not entirely surprised that he was looking aggrieved at her lack of interest. He was probably in for a fat commission for this sale.

'I'm not going to be rushed. I'll look them over in my own good time, Signor Bellini...'

'Stefano,' he suggested, with a smile that was manufactured out of glass and totally transparent.

Lili bit back the repeat of what she had said to Vittorio Rossi the day before. Very determinedly she stated, 'I'll let you know my decision at a later date. As I said, I've no intention of being rushed. Black or white coffee?'

His reply was drowned out by the deep rumble of an approaching truck up the dirt-track road.

'The water tanker,' Lili breathed in explanation, and Vittorio Rossi with it too, no doubt. She was relieved. She'd prefer Rossi's company to Bellini's, and that was some admittance.

'So you are staying for a while?' Bellini looked delighted at that and Lili guessed why. It would give him longer to persuade her to sell.

'For as long as it takes,' she told him tightly.

'I'm pleased,' he grinned, stretching out a hand to her in a farewell gesture, Lili hoped. 'It will give us a chance to get better acquainted,' he said meaningfully.

She took his moist hand briefly and then sucked it back out of reach. 'Yes, that would be nice,' she lied, because she was sensible enough to know that a buyer in the hand was worth more than two in the bush.

He beamed broadly at that. 'I'll look forward to seeing more of you, then, and a pleasure it will be too. I won't stay for the coffee, Lili—another time maybe, very soon.'

She walked with him to the front door as the tanker shuddered to a halt with a hiss of hydraulic brakes outside. A crazy thought ran through her as they went out into blinding sunlight. Stefano Bellini was flirting with her for the very same reason as Vittorio Rossi—for her father's house. The thought was only mildly amusing.

'What did he want?' were Vittorio Rossi's first words as he strode into the house.

Lili poured two coffees and then turned to him, her eyes flicking over his height with interest. This morning he was no Italian aristocrat in his stone-washed jeans and white T-shirt. The noise from rushing water into the deposit tank raised up from the ground outside was so deafening that she waited to give her reply.

He stepped closer to her and repeated impatiently, 'What did he want?'

She knew exactly who he meant. He obviously knew Stefano Bellini and must have seen him leaving, but she feigned innocence to annoy him.

'Who?'

'Bellini, of course, unless he wasn't the only man you've been entertaining so early this morning.'

'Who said anything about this morning?' she shouted over the noise, hoping he got the implication of that. Who did he think he was coming in here and making such suggestions?

He smiled thinly. 'You joke, of course?'

Her eyes widened innocently as if she weren't joking at all. The noise suddenly stopped and she heard his short breath and knew that her intention to annoy him had been a success.

'So what did he want?' he repeated, and the thin smile had vaporised away.

'Would you like a coffee? I've just poured you one.' She was really getting to him and it pleased her. He needed someone to bring his arrogance down.

'Yes, I would like a cup along with the answer to my question. What did Bellini want?' He went to the fridge for a carton of milk.

'He thought he would pay me a visit as he has a prospective purchaser for this property. But I expect you knew that anyway,' she told him tartly.

The fridge door crashed shut. 'He's wasting his time and you are wasting yours. I've already told you, I don't want this villa sold.'

Lili swallowed a shot of caffeine before she spoke again; she really needed it because this man was being quite ridiculous.

'I don't care what you want,' she said at last. 'Your wishes have nothing to do with it. *If* I decide to sell, I will, and I don't need your say-so.'

'But that is where you are wrong,' he informed her confidently. 'You will need my say-so, as you put it, but I will never give it, not so long as I have a breath left in my body.'

Lili's hand tightened around her coffee-cup. She leaned stiffly back against the work surface and glared back at him. For some reason her heart was racing as if she really believed he might have that sort of power. But it was bluff, of course. He was just trying to frighten her, but for what reason she had no idea.

'My father left me this house——'

'Exactly, this house.' His eyes locked into hers, loaded with confidence.

'What . . . what do you mean?' she whispered.

Vittorio Rossi put down his coffee-cup. 'The Villa Libra was once mine, part of my estate. I gave it to your father, a gift . . .'

Lili's heart began to thud. Now he was going to say he wanted that gift back!

'I had great respect for him,' he went on, 'and a great love too . . .' Lili's heart accelerated nervously. 'I enjoyed his company immensely and I would like to think that my feelings for him were returned. Your father would not have wanted this house sold. I know he wanted you to have it——'

'To teach me the values of life?' Lili cut in. Her pulses stopped racing and she hurt inside, so much. Her voice reduced to a whisper. 'For heaven's sake, what sort of a daughter did he think he had produced?'

The question hung sullenly in the air till Vittorio answered it quietly. 'He didn't know, Lili.'

Shakily Lili moved the coffee-cup to her lips and swallowed hard. Of course her father didn't know how she had turned out as a mature woman. He had only known the child. The thought deeply saddened her as it often had in the past when she was feeling low and vulnerable.

'He should have known,' she said at last, and then silence enfolded them once again.

'Why do you want to sell it?' he asked her after a long pause.

'I never said I did, not definitely.' She shrugged and studied the uneven tiles at her feet. 'I still don't know what I'm going to do, now that I'm here.'

'So why didn't you come sooner? Why wait for over two years to come?'

She raised her painful eyes to his. 'Because I couldn't come before,' she breathed in exasperation. 'I've been studying and working and trying to make a life for myself. I used to live with my mother but she was always on the move and then finally she moved to Scotland, so I had to find a place of my own. And . . . and . . .' She lowered her eyes again. They were all excuses really, so perhaps now was the time to be honest. 'And besides . . . I was afraid,' she admitted.

Vittorio Rossi stepped towards her and lifted her chin. 'Afraid of what?'

How could she tell him that she was afraid of what she would find here—the love-nest of her father and his mistress that had deprived her of her father and made her mother so bitter over the years?

She moved her head away from him and braved herself to look into his eyes. 'My mother stopped my visits when I was a child and by the time I grew up and could do something about it, it was too late. But all that's in the past now and . . . and the property is mine and I want to sell it.' She knew as she said it that it was true. She'd spent a night here, a strange night in which she hadn't even had the courage to open her father's study door and find out how he had lived his life over the years. 'Yes, I want to sell,' she told him more strongly now. 'I'm a textile designer and I want a studio of my own and the money from this sale will give me that freedom, and if my father was here now he would applaud that choice. So . . . so if you have any feelings for my father's last wishes you won't put blocks in my path.'

His hand came up and smoothed a tear from her cheek and anger filled her. He had made her cry and she hadn't even noticed.

'If I thought that your father would want that, I wouldn't put any blocks in your path, *cara*, but there is so much more to life than——'

'Earning a living?' she blazed back at him, brushing his fingers from her heated cheek. 'No, probably not to someone like you who delegates rather than gets his own hands dirty.' She glanced at his hands. They were strong and masculine but they hadn't pruned a vine in this life and wouldn't in the next.

'You have made a hasty decision,' he grated. 'I suggest you give it more thought.'

'What difference will it make?' she cried indignantly. 'You're going to stop me anyway, though how you think you can do that mystifies me.'

'There are ways but I would prefer not to implement them. I would much rather you decided against selling for reasons of the heart, not because of my threats.' His eyes held hers and mocked them.

Did he mean her heart for his? No way. He stood no chance of that happening. He had kissed her and what had that meant? Very little to a hot-blooded Italian, even less to her... but of course... he hadn't meant that at all and she was a silly fool to even give the thought brain space. He was referring to that sentimentality she ought to be feeling in her father's house.

His hand moved up to her cheek again and the soft caress he brushed down the side of her face melted her bones. Lili's eyes widened and then his mouth was on hers once again, sending her heart spinning. His lips were...exciting...but no, that wasn't possible. A man so arrogant as he couldn't excite, more like infuriate. His hands moved to pull her more strongly against him and the heat and the fire was there as before, astonishing her with its strength. She didn't want this but couldn't stop it. She balled her fists to her sides, terrified in case they worked of their own accord, circling around his neck and drawing him ever closer. But it was as if they had, because the kiss deepened, as if she had given her consent for it to go a dangerous stage further.

Danger—it was there, in a secret place deep inside her. To give in to a man such as this was dangerous, a man who was cold and insulting, a man who believed she had no sentiment, no values of life...a man who didn't want this house sold for reasons only he knew about...and a man she didn't even know.

Lili heard small running footsteps on the gravel outside and Vittorio Rossi stiffened against her. The pressure on her mouth grazed more heatedly as if somehow time was of the essence and then Lili's heart stopped as she heard a voice calling.

'Papà! Papà!'

Suddenly she and Vittorio were three feet apart as a small boy rushed into the long room and across to the kitchen. He stopped dead in his tracks as his father roared at him, 'I told you to stay in the car!'

Lili's head buzzed furiously as her heart pumped blood back into her veins.

'Lili?' the small boy cried in wonderment and then, ignoring his father, he threw himself into her waist.

'Carlo!' Lili breathed, her face white with shock as she hugged the boy to her, shocked at seeing him again and so terribly shocked that the child was the son of Vittorio Rossi.

To Lili's embarrassment the boy clung to her. She caught Vittorio Rossi's eyes as he darkly registered the embrace and her embarrassment turned to a rage of pain and fury. He was Carlo's father! He was married! And only seconds before the child had burst in she had been in his arms! He had tried to make love to her—this *papà* had kissed her sensuously, passionately and...and yes, she hated him for that, passionately!

CHAPTER THREE

CARLO released Lili and went to his father, who placed a restraining hand on his son's shoulder.

'I said I wouldn't be long and to wait in the car,' Vittorio said, his voice deep and throaty. Lili wondered if it was through guilt, though that wasn't much of a possibility—men such as him didn't suffer that way. 'Now do as you are told and go back.'

'But Papà, it's so hot and I'm——'

The grip on the boy's shoulder tightened and the boy fell silent. Lili came to her senses.

'You must be thirsty. I'll get you a drink.'

Carlo looked appealingly at his father who nodded his consent, at the same time giving Lili a murderous look.

The injustice of that! Lili turned away and poured the boy a drink, explaining hurriedly to his father, 'We met on the flight coming over...sat next to each other...struck up quite a friendship.'

'Papà, why is Lili——?'

Again Carlo was silenced, though Lili, with her back to them both, didn't know how that had been accomplished. A Chinese burn this time, no doubt! Her heart went out to the boy with a father so...what was the word she was seeking? Amoral was sufficient for the time being, though not nearly strong enough.

Carlo took the drink she offered, drank it in one, and handed the glass back to her, murmuring, '*Grazie*,' as he did it. Lili watched him in silence, not daring to raise her eyes to meet Vittorio's.

'Will you come on the picnic with us?' Carlo asked.

Lili and Vittorio both spoke at once with a positive, 'No.'

Lili hurriedly went on, 'I have a lot to do, Carlo.'

Vittorio said, equally hurriedly, 'Come, Carlo, we have a long drive ahead of us.'

'But Papà, why is Lili here? This house belongs to Nonno.' He said it so quickly that Vittorio had no time to silence him this time.

'It belongs to Lili now,' Vittorio said quickly as if anticipating an interruption himself. 'Now go outside and wait in the car for me.'

Carlo beamed at Lili. 'Good, I'm glad it's your house now. I can come and see you often.'

'Lili has no time for inquisitive boys,' Vittorio said hurriedly and Lili bit back a small protest. She would have loved his company but in the circumstances it wasn't a very good idea. 'Now go outside, Carlo.'

This time the boy obeyed and with a secret grin at Lili he raced back outside. Lili read that look; he knew he would be welcome if he called, no matter what his father said. But, endearing as he was, she didn't want it to happen.

She looked at Vittorio and didn't try to hide the bitterness at what he had done before the boy had burst in. Her eyes were cold and accusing.

'And what is a *nonno* when it's at home?' she asked sourly.

'It means grandfather...'

Lili suppressed a wild gasp, her mind spinning with the implications of that.

'But, as we both know, that isn't a fact,' he went on coolly. 'My son has no grandfather and your father was the nearest he had.'

Lili went hot and cold inside. The boy she had travelled with from England had had more of a relationship with her father than she had. The thought hurt so badly that she wanted to weep for those lost years. She wished she had never come, wished she had never met this Italian family with their close connections with her father.

'I see,' she murmured, too shocked to ask him how his wife was, which had been the next sarcastic question on her lips.

Vittorio stepped towards her and Lili held her breath as their eyes met. Why hadn't she seen the likeness between man and boy before? But she would never have made the connection—no, not in a million years. Dear God, if he made any attempt to touch her again she would die of the shame of it all.

'I must go now. I promised to take Carlo out for the day. I will call again but if you need anything——'

'Nothing!' she blurted, shaking her head from side to side. 'I need nothing!'

His eyes blazed for a split-second and she hated him even more for that. How dared he show anger to her after what he had done? He turned and walked away, and Lili closed her eyes, so sick that she felt faint with it.

She heard the car pull away with a spin of tyres on the gravel and only then did she breathe. Shakily she poured more coffee. Vittorio Rossi was married and the beautiful Carlo was his son, the stunning woman at the airport his wife. Were they happy? Perhaps not. Lili let out a cynical laugh at the walls. She hadn't been born yesterday. A man like him probably had a string of mistresses, and it had nothing to do with being unhappy with his wife. He probably loved her very much, just had too much fire in his rotten Italian loins!

Lili couldn't get him out of her mind, nor the boy Carlo. Life was so strange to throw up co-incidences like that. As the morning wore on Lili decided enough was enough. No more time wasted wondering about the Rossi family, otherwise nothing would get done. Well, there was one way of exorcising them from her mind and that was to occupy herself with her own family business, sorting out her father's belongings.

She went into his study and stood there for a very long time. So why hadn't Vittorio disposed of his things if he was such a great friend of his? He obviously thought there was no necessity as, according to him, the place wasn't going to be sold. But hadn't he said he had waited two years for her to come? Yes, it was her place to do any disposing of, and as she eventually moved listlessly round the room she knew she couldn't do that, not yet anyway. Touching his desk and his books was having a profoundly deep effect on her. Somehow all her father's writing paraphernalia belonged here . . .

Hot and uncomfortable, and for some reason irritable, she left the study and ran upstairs and stood outside her father's bedroom door, the room he had shared with . . . Emilia.

Tentatively Lili opened the door and it was as she imagined it would be. A lovers' room. There was lace and antique furniture, soft pale rugs on the tiled floor, water-colours on the white stone walls.

She slumped down on to the edge of the bed and gingerly picked up a silver-framed photo from the bedside table. Somehow Lili had always imagined a mistress to be young and nubile, especially a successful writer's mistress, but the face in the picture wasn't young. Nevertheless she was beautiful, in a soft and mature way. She was elegant too and very, very happy. Love shone out of her dark eyes and Lili felt an unaccustomed stab of jealousy knife through her. Not jealousy for the hold she'd had over her father but because Emilia had truly loved, spiritually. That was something Lili knew little about, true love, when the man in your life *was* your life, for now and forever and beyond death.

'So what have you been doing with yourself since last I was here?'

Lili had seen him coming down through the vineyards as she was feeding the stray cats that had suddenly appeared around the courtyard now that somebody was in residence. She fed them every day, titbits from her plate and milk and scraps of meat she brought up from the village.

Living, she wanted to say, but it would sound as if she was trying to cope, which was true but she didn't want him to know how she felt, which was very low. Here, in her father's love-nest, she felt she didn't really belong anywhere in the world.

'Adopting a few cats,' she told him, straightening up to look at him.

'And what is that?' Vittorio nodded towards the cardboard box at her feet filled with dried grass and weeds she'd gathered from the edge of the vineyards.

'A box, from the *mercato* in the village——'

'So, what is it for?'

'One of the cats is pregnant and I thought——'

He laughed drily. 'And you thought it would birth in that?'

'Why not?' she suggested hesitantly, feeling a little foolish for her concern over the pregnant cat who normally lived its life in the vineyards.

'You English are so sentimental with your animals; pity it doesn't extend to your relatives.'

Lili took the blow on her chin as if it had been physically thrown.

'Look to your own before passing judgement on others,' she retorted bitingly when she had recovered.

Anger glinted Vittorio's eyes. 'And what exactly do you mean by that?'

Lili went to walk away but he swung her back to face him, his eyes glittering darkly now. Lili lowered hers to his hand gripping her arm and glared at it disdainfully.

'Please don't restrain me that way. I'm not a seven-year-old child to be silenced by force.'

'And what exactly do you mean by *that*?' he said harshly.

'Is that your stock phrase for the day? You've said it enough times.'

'And I'll say it again till I get what I want,' he threatened. 'Were you implying that I use force on my son?'

Lili wrenched her arm from his grasp. 'Yes, I was implying just that. When Carlo rushed into the house last time you were here you couldn't wait to silence him, and understandable it was too! The last thing you wanted was for me to know you had a wife and son!' She turned and walked back to the wooden door that led to the inner courtyard.

She was nearly to the laundry-room before she realised he was right behind her and chuckling too. She swung furiously.

'That's funny to you, is it?' she cried angrily. 'I see nothing funny or clever in a married man trying to seduce another woman!'

He stood by the fig tree, one hand on an upper branch, one thumb caressing the smooth bark, one mouth grinning widely.

'It isn't funny,' he agreed to her fury. 'Your re-action is. Very amusing.'

'Because I object to what you did to me the other day?' she asked in astonishment at his arrogance.

'Kissed you?' he asked rhetorically. 'You didn't object when I did it.'

Oh, she had; her very soul had screamed out her objection, but her heart, for some extraordinary reason, had overruled it.

'I didn't know you were married then!'

'Which goes to prove how very careful you need to be these days. It's better to ask questions before, not after. After could be too late.'

Too late indeed if you had already lost your heart. Fortunately she hadn't, so what harm had been done? She didn't know, but she felt some sort of let-down, some sort of hurt. But no, not hurt, simply indignation at his loose morality, expecting hers to be similarly tuned.

'For once I agree with you, Vittorio Rossi; better to know before the event than after.'

'"The event" being a euphemism for sex?' he suggested with a wry twist of his mouth.

Lili *touchéd* smartly with, 'And the word sex itself a euphemism.'

He laughed again and it gave Lili no pleasure to know that she could amuse him so easily. 'I think we had better change the subject before this conversation gets down to gutter level,' he suggested lightly.

'Yes, I quite understand why you should use that cliché,' she went on, not ready to relinquish this line of conversation before she'd had her full say. 'That's what adultery is all about.'

'We haven't committed adultery,' he said smoothly, still obviously amused.

'But you wish it,' she said hotly. 'Otherwise why the kiss? One thing leads to another. A kiss today, bed tomorrow.'

'I see the world has progressed alarmingly without me all these years——'

'Oh, don't come all puritanical with me, Vittorio Rossi,' Lili stormed. 'The Romans invented the orgy, don't forget!'

His eyes were bright with amusement. 'What a legacy for us to live up to.'

'And you do!' She turned, flew into the house and would have slammed the door in his face if it weren't wedged open with a stone. She knew he was close behind her; she felt his presence and hated herself for the awareness it aroused in her.

'Look, why are you here again?' she asked wearily as she washed her hands at the sink. 'Put that down!' she ordered as he picked up her sketch pad from the kitchen chair.

He ignored her. 'You have a good eye for colour,' he complimented, turning the pad this way and that.

'And you obviously haven't for perspective,' she said flatly, twisting the pad the right way up for him.

He smiled. 'Ah, yes, I see now. The bougain-villaea. So much beauty yet such an insignificant flower.'

'Insignificant? Hardly—it's very exotic,' Lili muttered, drying her hands.

Vittorio shook his head. 'A common mistake. The bracts are not the flower—the flower is small and insignificant inside and there is no perfume for such a rich display of colour. Very misleading. Like so much in life, it isn't what it seems.' His eyes pierced into hers as if they held some hidden message.

'And people aren't what they seem either,' she retorted, getting the message in one.

He nodded agreement with a smile creasing his mouth. 'Exactly. I think I made a mistake with you. Passed judgement on you before the trial.'

His voice was smooth and velvety and Lili was on alert. Now he was going softly, softly with her, trying to make up for his rudeness at their first meeting and the fact that he was a married man who'd made a pass at her and was about to make another one.

She moved away from him to the fridge—better safe than sorry. 'As you said, you have to be careful these days, and I'm glad you see the mistake you made with me.'

'What mistake is that?'

'All of them.' She opened the fridge and took out a carton of juice. 'Would you like some?'

'Juice?'

Of course juice, she wanted to cry, not anything else. She poured two glasses and told him firmly, 'I'm not out to make a killing with the sale of this house and you were very wrong to believe that that was my intention when I came here, and you don't know the reason why I didn't attend my father's funeral——'

'So are you going to tell me now?'

'No, it's personal.'

'A man in your life?'

'That's rich coming from a man who secretes the knowledge of his wife and child from his latest sexual target!' she retorted bitterly, her back to him as she placed the juice carton back in the fridge. 'My personal life is just that—personal; now, to get back to what I was saying.' Lili turned then because facing him would add weight to what she was going to say. 'You were also very wrong in thinking I was free with my emotions.' She handed him one of the glasses of orange juice. 'I don't mess around with married men,' she added sincerely.

'I'm glad to hear that.' He dropped her pad back on to the chair and took the glass she offered. 'So you had better not mess with Stefano Bellini.'

Lili couldn't help a small splutter of indignation. 'I fail to see what Stefano Bellini has to do with this!'

'He is a married man and quite an attractive one to some women, and he plays the field hard, regardless of his wife and two small children at home. He has the morals of an alley cat.' He said it as a warning and Lili was quite appalled that he could issue it as such after what he himself had done.

'Amazing,' she breathed in disbelief. 'Well, it takes one to know one! Thanks for the information. I'll keep it mind when next he corners me in the alley.'

Vittorio Rossi drained his juice in one gulp and Lili noticed his hand was gripping the glass so tightly it whitened his knuckle. He put the empty glass down before saying, 'So he has already made an advance to you?'

'I . . . I didn't say that.'

'When next, you said; that is enough for me.' His eyes narrowed. 'Be very careful, Lili. Stefano might have wholesome good looks but he's the devil himself.'

Lili lifted her chin defiantly and smiled cynically. 'Really? That makes him sound far more exciting than he appeared and it's interesting that you are both powered by the same reason for trying to mess with my emotions.'

'I doubt that very much.'

'And no doubt he would say the very same thing!'

Vittorio shook his dark head and smiled. 'I am powered by my heart, which isn't always a good thing; Stefano is powered by greed; that is always a bad thing.'

'I think you are a liar, Vittorio Rossi. You have no heart. You tried to seduce me for the very same reason Stefano Bellini might if I gave him half a chance. You both want this house. His reason is glaringly obvious—a chunk of commission and fees for the transaction. Your reasons I haven't quite worked out yet, but give me time—and in that time I would be grateful if you both kept away from me, because that is the other thing you have in common—you are both married!'

He caught her before she stormed through to the long room, swung her into his arms. His mouth was on hers before she had a chance to cry out. In that agonisingly revealing second Lili knew and understood the weakness in women having an affair with a married man. One kiss, in spite of all she knew about him, was enough to have her heart hammering wildly, her blood frothing dangerously. She tried to pull away but his arms locked tightly around her and yet were incredibly sensuous as they smoothed down her back to grasp her ever tighter to him. She felt the wild beat of his own heart and recognised his weakness too. Yes, he had a heart and was powered by it now, but a foolish heart that deceived him so treacherously by inflaming a need he had no right to exercise.

She tore her mouth from his. 'Is . . . is that a test? Your ego test, to prove that your machismo can push me to do something so despicable!'

He still held her tightly against him and looked down into her flushed face. There was deep desire in his hooded eyes and she hated him for that. A cruel smile creased the corners of his mouth. 'And you are being pushed, aren't you? Temptation bites.'

She shook her head determinedly. 'You are out of order, very much mistaken——'

'I am not mistaken, *cara*. Your heart beats like a caged bird's wings, panicking for release to be free. You want what I want; let me prove it.' He took her hand and Lili's pulses froze at what he might do with it!

There was relief as he held her hand to his own heart, but only a temporary relief. 'Hear it—the beat of a heart that wants more than a kiss—and your heart beats out the same need.'

'You bastard,' Lili breathed.

'For finding you so desirable? If that is so, so be it, a *bastardo* I am.'

She struggled but he held on to her. 'You are not a bastard because of your desire but a bastard for allowing it. That poor boy——'

He laughed. 'My son is far from poor, in means or love, but that is a very interesting thought that your heart is so concerned for him and no one else.'

'Your wife, you mean? Well, my heart bleeds for her too, but I'm sure she can handle the likes of you—she's probably had enough practice; but remember one thing: the child is the one to suffer when a marriage goes wrong.'

'As you know,' he murmured, lifting one hand to graze her silky hair from her brow. She thought she would be free when restrained by only one hand but in that one hand he had the power of ten men and she wriggled hopelessly.

'Yes, I know!' she hissed through tight lips, fury masking the hurt. 'I had no father because of the break-up of my parents' marriage and I'm not dredging for sympathy but——'

'But that was no fault of his mistress. The marriage was over before Emilia——'

'And that has nothing to do with what is happening here,' she burst out indignantly.

'It poses an interesting theory, though.'

Slowly his arms slackened and Lili was suddenly free. She stepped back and breathed deeply, her small breasts rising and falling as if she had run a mile. She was shaking too, trembling with the shock of his physical and verbal onslaught.

'And what theory is that?' She really didn't want to know but the words just came, probably to show that she wasn't at all shaken by his ruthless lovemaking—except she was.

He folded the arms that had just held her so forcibly across his chest. 'The theory that if a love is great enough it overrides wives and husbands. Who knows what would have happened between Hugo and Emilia if they were still married to others?'

'My father would never have had an affair and...and I can't speak for Emilia because I didn't know her but...but if she was...was married when they met my father would never, never have got himself into that situation,' Lili argued. She knew that with a fierce certainty and she despised this man for suggesting otherwise.

'She wasn't married,' he told her reassuringly, recognising her hurt immediately. 'She was a widow when your father met her, but who are we, as outsiders looking in, to judge what would have happened if they hadn't been free to love?'

Lili turned away and reached for her drink, her other hand coming up to knead her brow. She really didn't know the answer to that one.

'I wouldn't know,' she breathed after gulping at her drink. 'I've never been in love.' But somehow she could understand. She had felt the past love of those two people in this house. It seeped out from the walls. Yes, a love like that could overcome all, but why should she suddenly understand that?

Painfully she raised her eyes to look at him and knew the danger she was in. Here stood before her a man she hardly knew who, though married, had raised all sorts of problems inside her. He was attractive, nearly charismatic, strangely and oddly romantic, and he had...excited her. The excitement she had so longed for in her life. But no; that was before she knew about Carlo.

'I fail to see where this conversation is going or the point of it,' she uttered, suddenly wanting to be out in fresh air. She stepped out of the kitchen to the laundry-room and through to the courtyard, sat down at the rustic table and stared blindly at the bougainvillaea drooping down from the walls.

'It was an interesting conversation nevertheless,' he said quietly behind her. 'At least, it interested me, and what led to it was even more interesting.'

'I don't know what you mean.'

He sat across from her, the shade of the vines adding even more depth to his eyes. 'You believed

me to be married and yet your heart beat wildly
when I kissed you; don't you find that interesting?'

'I would find it *disgusting* if it were the truth. A
heart can race wildly for many different reasons,
fear being one of them.'

'So you were afraid; that is even more
interesting.'

'I didn't say I was afraid.'

'Why mention it, then?'

'It was just a suggestion, and why are you
pushing me like this?' She couldn't see where it was
leading.

'Because I want to know the depth of your
feelings for me——'

'I haven't any!' she retorted hotly.

'But you have. I excite you.'

Her face coloured deeply and she was glad of the
shade that offered some protection.

'You're married!'

'And yet I still excite you and you are still afraid,
not of me but of yourself.'

'Don't be ridiculous! I'm not at all afraid of
myself.'

'Because you don't know yourself. Has there ever
been a man in your life?'

'What the hell——?'

'You see, you are afraid. You protest before
giving it any thought. Are you afraid to love?'

'Of course not! I haven't met anyone——'

'Anyone who excites you enough for love,' he
finished for her.

She stared at him incredulously. How could he
know? She shook her head. 'No, there is more to
love than excitement.'

'But that is where it starts, *cara*. The pulsing of the heart, the fire in the loins—that is where love begins and that is what interests me about you. I kiss you and hold you and am not mistaken in what I get back from you, and that is a very good basis for an ongoing relationship.'

'Are you crazy?' she breathed heatedly, her eyes widening at him. 'Are you completely and utterly out of your mind? My pulses don't race and I have no fire in my loins for you!'

'Your delectable mouth speaks the words but your body betrays you. I know, *cara*. I know what you feel when I take you in my arms and I know what I feel too—the same need as your own.'

'You are mad,' Lili crazed, almost stupefied by his arrogance. 'You don't even like me. You started all this because you thought you could win me over enough to stop me selling my father's house——'

'Never that, *cara*. I couldn't possibly make love to you without desiring you. I didn't like you before you arrived. I'd built up some image of a heartless soul who had shown no interest in her father——'

'And you don't know any differently now,' Lili retorted.

'No, I don't, but I desire you, so you can't be all bad.' His eyes contained humour now, soft brown like warm chocolate. 'Now let us get back to your quickening heartbeat.'

'What quickening heartbeat?' Lili cried. 'The one that keeps popping up in your imagination as often as your libido does in real life?'

He smiled, having fun. 'No imagination where your heartbeat is concerned. I wasn't mistaken, the first time nor the second. Don't deny it, Lili.'

'OK, I won't deny it. I'll admit to it, then perhaps you'll leave me in peace, but let me put you straight. I got a buzz the first time but this time it was definitely a negative zap.'

'Because I am married?'

'Of course because you are married!'

'And yet still the pulses raced.'

'A reflex action, out of my control!' she blazed back at him.

'And you are really angry about that, aren't you?'

'Yes . . . yes, I am, not only angry but not particularly proud of it.'

'So let's gather up all the pieces of this very interesting conversation. You feel something for me, you want what I want but you are held back because of my wife and son?'

'No . . . I mean . . .' Her eyes flamed wildly, trapped. 'Look, you are a very attractive man, physically. Your character needs polishing but . . . if I had met you . . . anywhere else but here . . . at a party . . . and you were single . . .'

'You would allow me into your heart?'

'It . . . it could have happened,' she uttered weakly. Yes, she would be attracted to him, she admitted to herself as reluctantly as she admitted that he excited her, and she could safely make those admissions now because the situation was a no-go. 'But it is impossible. You're a married man with a beautiful son——'

'Praise the child and love the father,' he murmured with satisfaction honeying his voice, humour glinting his eyes again.

'I don't see what you have to look so self-satisfied about,' she stabbed back, 'and the proverb is

''Praise the child and love the mother'', not the father.'

He leaned back in his seat and looked so very pleased with himself that she wanted to scream. OK, so she had admitted her attraction to him, but she had nothing to lose because it was going nowhere— it *couldn't* go anywhere!

'But you see, *cara*, there *is* no mother, only the father.' The statement came slowly and levelly, delivered with such deadly intent that it made her heart race further than it had ever raced before. 'So, you see, there is no reason for this not to be an ongoing relationship. No wife, no problem.'

Slowly he stood up and smoothed his jeans down over his thighs, a gesture so wretchedly sexual that she swallowed hard, wishing the very earth would open beneath her and take her to a safer place than this.

He moved towards where she sat as motionless as a stone and brushed a kiss across her forehead, then drooped his mouth to her burning lips. This kiss was so very different. No more a temptation but simply a statement of fact that he would get his way, whatever that might be.

CHAPTER FOUR

'THIS is a ridiculously large amount of money,' Lili told Stefano Bellini a week later. A week in which the world had disappeared. No one had called so when Stefano had turned up half an hour ago she'd actually been glad to see him; now she couldn't wait to be rid of him. The amount of money this client of his was offering was so grossly inflated as to be suspicious, and as the minutes ticked by Bellini was getting more impatient and irate.

'The purchaser is willing to pay it, so what's the big deal?' He helped himself to another glass of fizzy Lambrusco and leaned back under the shade of the vine to knock it back as swiftly as the three previous glasses.

'The big deal is why the purchaser is willing to pay so much for a property up here in the back of beyond, and I would have thought he or she might have shown enough interest to come here and negotiate directly with me.'

'I'm acting as his agent.'

'You are, are you? Then I would have thought it would be in your client's interest for you to negotiate the price *down*, not *up*!'

Lili's eyes challenged his for an answer to that. His face coloured hotly and that confirmed all Lili's suspicions. This was all more than it appeared.

'What's going on here?' she breathed hotly. 'Who is this client of yours wishing to get me out of my father's house—at any price?'

'Me,' he said simply, and raised the glass to his lips yet again.

'You?' Lili scorched. 'What an earth would you want this house for?' Stefano Bellini didn't appear the sort to appreciate beauty and living in an area that had nothing else to offer but its setting.

'I just want it,' he shrugged. Suddenly he looked across at her. 'Has Vittorio Rossi tried to persuade you not to sell?'

She hadn't seen him for a week. Not since he had told her there was no mother for Carlo. He'd left her with that. No explanations as to why or how he was a single parent. Bellini would most likely know but she didn't want to ask him. She wanted Vittorio to tell her himself—that was if he ever decided to come back into her life. So he had no wife—so who was that gorgeous creature who'd picked Carlo up from the airport? Certainly not the local minicab service!

'And why should he be interested in stopping me selling?'

Stefano shrugged. 'He's a weirdo, that's all. Lives in the past. This scheme I have for the area will bring prosperity——'

'What scheme?' Lili murmured, 'No, don't tell me. You want to develop the area into a theme park for purple giraffes and Rossi is green and wants to carry on growing grapes in the age-old way as his forefathers did before him. Excuse me while I yawn.'

Stefano made no comment to that, which made Lili think she had come close to the truth. He drained his glass and stood up, and Lili didn't stop him.

'I'd like to take you out to dinner,' Stefano suddenly said when they reached the front door.

'Really? And what would your wife say if I accepted?' Lili queried with a knowing smile hovering around her lips. What on earth did he take her for? The same as Vittorio Rossi—a push-over?

'Who told you I was married?' Suddenly he smiled. 'Who else?' he muttered thickly. 'Well, don't forget he is too.'

Lili's stomach tightened. 'But...'

Stefano laughed cynically. 'But you thought he wasn't?' He shook his head. 'She might not be in evidence but she is still very much with him and always will be. No woman can ever take her place though many have tried. He has a son too——'

'Yes, I know,' Lili interjected quickly, drawing the back of her hand across her forehead. 'We've met.'

Stefano raised a brow and stopped at the doorway. Lili thought he was going to say something about Carlo but he simply grinned and said, 'I'd still like to take you out to dinner. No need to be old-fashioned about these things...'

'Goodbye, Stefano,' Lili said coldly. 'I know where to get hold of you when I come to my decision—about the house, that is!'

'Oh, I'll be back,' Stefano laughed, wagging an infuriating finger at her. 'Just try and keep me away.'

Lili slammed the door after him and leaned back against it, taking deep breaths to calm herself. Was the world full of married men chasing single women? And all those things Stefano had said about Vittorio—were they true? Was he a weirdo, living in the past, and did he still have a wife, maybe one who had left him?

'Carlo!' Lili croaked in surprise as the boy rushed into the house from the courtyard outside. She heaved herself away from the back of the door and went across the room to him.

The boy hugged her. 'Papà and Christina are coming by car. I ran down through the vines because it's my favourite way. Christina doesn't walk in the heat of the day. We want you to come to dinner.' He was so excited that the words tumbled out of his mouth.

'Christina?' Lili laughed outwardly though inside her stomach was jelly on a moving escalator. Was she the woman who had picked Carlo up from the airport?

'Christina—she lives with us and looks after us. Can I have a drink, please?' He didn't wait for an answer but rushed to the fridge. Lili's heart felt like the inside of it—cold and frosty. So Christina lived with Vittorio. Not only did he have a wife but a live-in lover too! It was surprising he had time to flirt with her!

'Can I have a fizzy drink?' he asked breathlessly.
'Are you allowed it?'
'Sometimes,' the boy murmured, suddenly hesitant. 'Papà prefers me to drink water...will you come to dinner? I want you to come.'

'I . . . I don't know, Carlo.' Lili was now hesitant. She didn't want to get involved; she just didn't. Somehow Stefano's dinner invitation suddenly held more appeal, and that was admitting to something pretty grim!

She heard the car on the gravel as she was pouring the drink for Carlo. There was no polite knock on the door, just Vittorio Rossi pushing it open as if he owned it and its contents. The lovely woman from the airport followed him closely into the room, those dark, sultry eyes flashing around the long room with the avaricious look of a hunter searching for prey.

Lili herself was the final resting-place of her predatory eyes. Lili stood transfixed, paralysed by that look and feeling distinctly subhuman in her grimy shorts and baggy T-shirt. She'd been doing some weeding around the villa when Stefano had arrived and was looking far from her best. Christina wasn't. She was beautifully dressed in a bright silk dress of cerise that was vibrant against her glowing olive skin. Lili's first thought was of the exotic bougainvillaea. The woman smiled at last and Lili was reminded of Vittorio's words: so much beauty yet such a deceptive appearance. The smile was the flower, small and very insignificant.

Vittorio made the introductions but failed to state her relationship with the Rossi family, and then Christina spoke, in excellent English of course. 'So you are the Lili Carlo talks about so often.' She said it as if she wondered what all the fuss was about.

'I'm flattered that Carlo thinks so highly of me,' Lili told her, not extending a smile in her direction, which she thought was probably a give-away omission on her part. Vittorio eyed her curiously.

'Carlo, did you ask for that drink? What have you been taught about fizzy drinks——?' Christina snapped at the boy.

'I offered it,' Lili cut in, instantly coming to the defence of him to save any embarrassment. 'And may I offer you a drink too?' she added politely.

Vittorio thanked her and she went to the wine-rack. 'Which one?' she asked, turning slightly. Vittorio was almost on top of her and she jerked at the close contact. He was smiling and his eyes danced; he stood so close that she knew he was doing it to unnerve her. His hand snaked past her and lifted a bottle of Sangiovese from the rack.

'This one.' His breath fanned her cheek as he moved away from her. Lili caught the swift averting of Christina's eyes. She had seen but didn't want it known that she had, but she couldn't disguise the slight pursing of her lips.

Lili sighed silently and laid a tray with glasses and the wine. Christina hadn't liked Vittorio's teasing familiarity and that made Lili feel more awkward than ever. They all went out into the shady courtyard. The two dirty glasses and the almost empty wine bottle were still on the table from Stefano's visit. Interesting, Lili thought as she pushed them aside to put the tray down. Vittorio had noted them and he wasn't very good at hiding his annoyance either. Lili wondered if Christina had registered the thinning of his lips as well.

'We would like you to come to dinner tonight,' Vittorio said after pouring the drinks for everyone.

Lili wondered who the 'we' encompassed.

'Yes, Carlo said. How very neighbourly,' Lili said sweetly. 'Thank you but——'

'Oh, you must come!' Carlo insisted. 'I want you to.'

Christina didn't want, that was for sure, Lili mused as she watched her looking disdainfully around the courtyard. Lili had left little piles of limp weeds on the cobbles to be swept up later. Christina must think this was how she lived, swigging wine all day and living in a tip.

'I will collect you, of course,' Vittorio offered. 'I don't expect you to walk up through the vineyards or take the rough road.'

'That wasn't my excuse for not wanting to come. It's just that——'

'It's just what?' Vittorio urged.

Suddenly three sets of eyes were focused on her, waiting for her excuse to be delivered. Of them all Lili was only certain that one set of eyes prayed that her excuse would be worthy enough to satisfy Vittorio—Christina's.

Lili smiled and shrugged; what had she got to lose? 'It's nothing. Thank you, yes, I'd like to come.'

Carlo shrieked and jumped in the air. Vittorio looked pleased, Christina looked peeved.

'Papà says you are a wonderful artist, Lili. Can I see your pictures?'

'I'm hardly an artist in the true sense,' Lili smiled at him, flattered that Vittorio thought so highly of her work. 'I design furnishing fabric. My pad's on the sofa; you can look through it if you want to but it's only plants and flowers.'

'Bring it out, Carlo,' Vittorio told his son. 'I'd be interested to see what Lili has been doing since we last met.' His dark, brooding eyes locked on the earlier discarded wine bottle partnered by the two wine glasses then flicked to her, leaving her in no doubt what he supposed she had been doing.

Carlo came back out to the courtyard with her pad and he and Vittorio pored over the mass of drawings she had worked on all week. Christina glanced briefly at them but then turned her attention to Lili.

'Your first visit to Tuscany?'

Lili nodded and sipped her wine.

'And how long are you staying?'

'I don't know yet,' Lili answered truthfully. 'I've got quite settled and it will be hard to tear myself away.' She wondered if Christina knew she was the daughter of Hugo Mayer and this was her villa now.

'But you'll have to go back, of course,' Christina said crisply. 'There's nothing here for you——'

'There's this house,' Vittorio interjected. 'And with a talent like this Lili could free-lance and earn enough to keep herself.'

So Christina must know, and there was Vittorio offering her an excuse to stay. Lili suspected the reason for that unrealistic suggestion was so that the house stayed unsold.

Christina gave a brittle laugh. 'Don't be ridiculous, Vittorio. Why should a pretty girl like Lili want to bury herself up here among the vineyards? And, besides, I'm sure she has a boyfriend at home waiting for her.'

Lili sat mute and Vittorio eyed her with interest, waiting for a reaction from her, but she wasn't going

to give one, because she knew why Christina had
made the suggestion—to find out if she was free to
contest for Vittorio Rossi's attentions. Good God,
life with these two must be wall-to-wall fun!

'You could marry Papà and live with us,' Carlo
burst out excitedly.

Christina was the only one who didn't laugh at
that. Vittorio and Lili did because the idea was pre-
posterous. Lili knew instantly why Christina didn't
find the idea rib-cracking. Her relationship with
Vittorio was tentative; it must be if she saw the
suggestion as a threat to her status with him.

Lili poured more wine and relaxed. So Stefano
had lied; Vittorio's wife wasn't with him, not in
body, that was. Carlo would never have made such
a remark if she had been; nor would he if his father
and Christina were in the throes of a relationship.
All surmise, of course; she knew none of this for
sure, but what she did know was that Christina was
madly in love with Vittorio.

Carlo moved away from the table and Christina
drew closer to Vittorio, feigning interest in Lili's
work just because Vittorio was finding it so fasci-
nating. She sat so close that there was barely a
whisper of air between them in the stifling heat and
she purposely brushed her hand across his as she
turned the pages. And Vittorio... To Lili's
amazement he seemed oblivious to it all.

Vittorio asked Lili questions about her work and
Christina tried to look interested at her replies and
they passed a pleasant few minutes till Vittorio suddenly said, 'Where's Carlo?'

Christina's guilty leap to her feet was all Lili
needed to guess where the lovely woman stood in

the Rossi household—nanny with delusions of grandeur, which Lili supposed marriage to Vittorio Rossi might appear to be to some.

'It's all right,' Lili said, getting to her feet. 'He went through to the other courtyard. I'll make sure he doesn't wander away.'

Lili was surprised at the rise in colour on Christina's face but maybe it had something to do with the way Vittorio looked displeased at her suggestion that she would look out for Carlo. It confirmed what Lili had supposed. Christina was Carlo's nanny and more interested in the father than the son, so that sometimes she forgot her position.

Lili froze as she stepped into the outer courtyard. Carlo was there, his hand raised high above his head. In a split-second Lili's widened eyes took in the whole scenario. Small boy, stone in clenched fist, cowering cat.

'Carlo!' Lili screamed, and the boy spun, but not before the stone had been flung against a clump of shrubbery where the tabby cat was cowering, ears flattened to the side of its head, the fur along its back spiky and stiff with fear.

The stone thumped wide of the cat but it scurried off none the less, disappearing into the vineyards. Lili recognised it as the pregnant cat and her anger rose.

She gripped Carlo's shoulders fiercely. 'Don't you ever ... don't you ever do that again ...'

'Carlo!' came a roar from Vittorio, then suddenly Carlo was wrenched out of her hands by a furious Christina.

'And don't you ever strike this boy again!' Christina screamed.

Lili clenched her fists at her side to stop them making contact with Christina's neck.

'I did not strike him, but I will not tolerate cruelty to animals——'

'Cruelty?' Vittorio grazed, looking from one to the other of the inflamed trio facing him, wondering what the hell was going on.

Lili stayed mute; a sneak she wasn't, a sneak Christina was.

'You are the cruel one, lashing out at our beloved Carlo!' she directed furiously at Lili.

Since when was Carlo her 'beloved'? Lili wondered. She remembered the cool indifference of the woman she had thought to be his mother when she had picked him up at the airport.

'I do not strike children,' Lili insisted, her face pale with the shock of what was going on.

'She didn't, Papà. Lili didn't hit me...' Carlo twisted out of Christina's arms and ran to his father, clutching at his hand and gazing up at him with wide eyes. 'I didn't mean to hit the cat...just to frighten it away... Christina does it...she kicks too...'

Lili let out an appalled exclamation. Christina flushed hotly and Vittorio's eyes darkened threateningly.

Christina broke into defensive Italian to which Vittorio ordered her to stop immediately. Carlo twisted his face into his father's side and started to cry quietly. Lili didn't know what to say or do.

'The cats are vermin, Vittorio,' Christina protested. 'You do not want them around the house...'

'Leave us for a while, Christina,' Vittorio said dully. 'Wait in the car.'

Humbly, Christina turned away but not before giving Lili a piercing look as if all this were her fault. No one spoke till she had gone, then it was Vittorio who spoke gently to his son.

'There is no need to cry, Carlo.' Vittorio looked at Lili. 'Would you like to tell me what is going on here?'

Lili shook her head and lowered her eyes, feeling only marginally older than little Carlo.

Carlo snuffled and slid the back of his hand across his nose. 'I was...I was throwing stones...not *at* the cats...' His eyes flickered to Lili. 'I wouldn't do that...not hurt them...I threw the stones to the side of them. I just wanted to frighten them away from the house. Christina says they are bad and smell and we mustn't let them into the house. Lili caught me and...she thought...she thought I was hurting them.'

'I'm sorry, Carlo,' Lili murmured regretfully. God, if only she had waited, just held back for a second longer, but her reactions had been instinctive. She really couldn't abide cruelty to animals. 'I must have frightened you when I grabbed you like that but...' Her eyes appealed to Vittorio for understanding. 'I can't bear to see animals hurt; I just can't bear it. One of the cats is pregnant...'

'It's having a baby?' Carlo cried, his eyes wide and moist, like limpid pools in a dark forest.

Lili smiled. 'Cats have kittens,' she told him gently, 'several, and hers will come soon and she needs to be quiet, not to be frightened by stones.'

'I didn't know,' Carlo said mournfully. 'Oh, I wish I hadn't done it. Will she come back? If she does, can I stay and watch them being born?'

'They're not coming that soon,' Lili laughed.

'When they do, can I watch? I'll come every day till it's time,' he blurted excitedly.

'I don't know,' Lili uttered, not knowing what to say. She looked at Vittorio for guidance but he gave her nothing but a deep look that she didn't understand.

'I think you should apologise to Lili,' Vittorio suggested. 'She has been looking after the cats so they are hers now.'

'I'm sorry,' Carlo cried, coming to her and throwing his arms around her waist. 'I'll never do it again; even if Christina does, I won't.'

Lili put her arms around him and smiled at Vittorio over the boy's head. She was sure he didn't mean to condemn Christina so.

'And I'm sorry for frightening you by shouting at you so fiercely, Carlo.' Lili smeared the last remnant of a tear from the boy's cheek and leaned down to kiss the top of his forehead. 'Friends again?'

Carlo reached up and pulled her down and kissed her on the cheek. 'We'll always be friends and you won't ever go back to England because if you do the cats won't have anyone to look after them, will they?'

'Carlo, why don't you go and tell Christina to drive you home? I'll walk back through the vineyards,' Vittorio said in a tone that ordered rather than suggested.

Carlo looked sullen and then sighed as his father cleared his throat in warning.

'OK, but I'd rather go with you than Christina. I hate Christina!' He turned and was about to run rebelliously out of the courtyard when Lili, without giving any serious thought that she might be interfering, grabbed at him.

'Just a minute, Carlo. I've got something for you.' She took hold of his hand and led him into the house, Vittorio following close behind.

Lili picked up a book from a table in the long sitting-room. She'd found it in the study. It was one her father had given her many years ago. She remembered she had left it behind in France on one of her visits. Now she regretted it because her father must have thought she hadn't wanted it.

She handed the book to Carlo. 'I want you to have this, Carlo. My father...' Vittorio made a small sound in his throat and Lili looked up to see him narrowing his eyes in warning to her. Lili's heart stilled. It was obvious that Carlo didn't know his *nonno* was her father but he probably knew this book belonged to Hugo; maybe her father had read him passages from it. 'My... my father gave me ... gave me one like it when I was small. It's one of my favourites. *The Wind in the Willows*—it's about animals, and they have feelings too. You can read it yourself or ask Christina to read it to you.' It might teach her a thing or two, Lili omitted to say.

'It's lovely,' Carlo enthused, clutching it to his chest. 'My very best book. Look, Papà, isn't it a lovely book?' He thrust it towards his father.

Vittorio looked down at his son's shining face and the book clutched in his hand and then he looked up at Lili, but the look he gave her wasn't as open as Carlo's. 'A very nice present,' he said unenthusiastically. 'Now thank Lili properly and go home with Christina.'

'Thank you very much, *Grazie, molto grazie,*' Carlo said politely and turned and ran out of the door.

'You shouldn't have given Carlo the book,' Vittorio grated as soon as he was out of sight and earshot. 'He was naughty——'

'He wasn't,' Lili insisted coldly. 'He was doing what he's been taught to do—to throw stones at defenceless cats.'

'He said he didn't mean——'

'I know what he said and I believe him. He didn't mean to hurt them but he could have done. If the stone...' Lili passed her hand over her forehead. She really didn't need this in this heat. 'Look, it's over with, no harm done. I gave Carlo the book because I wanted to, not as some sort of bribery to be good in future.'

'Your father gave you that book,' Vittorio said darkly. 'I would have thought it meant something to you.'

He was implying it didn't and that hurt Lili yet again but she wouldn't show it. 'It does,' Lili sighed wearily, 'but I'm a big girl now and I wanted Carlo to have it. He's a charming child.'

'Trying to ingratiate yourself into my favour by flattering my son?'

Though he was smiling now, she wasn't sure if it was mockingly or not. She took no chances.

'Why should I try that?' she said sweetly. 'I have no wish to be *in* your favour.'

'Ah, but it's a good idea to be in the favour of my son; through his heart you could eventually capture mine.'

Lili laughed at that. 'Really, what a very interesting theory,' she said sarcastically. 'Pure fantasy, of course. I'm not hunting hearts, I just happen to like your son, and of course I have a great sympathy towards him—he too comes from a broken home. Kindred spirits, you might say.'

'But Carlo does not come from a broken home,' Vittorio smoothed, 'not in the sense you mean.'

'And what sense do you think I mean?'

'A divorce-type broken home.'

'Are you divorced?' For some reason Lili held her breath in anticipation of his answer.

'No,' he said dully. 'I am not divorced. I do not believe in it.'

So Stefano was right, not wrong. Vittorio had a wife, though not in evidence, but nevertheless still with him in name.

'That must disappoint Christina,' Lili retorted, getting her own back on the woman who had falsely accused her of striking Carlo.

'What do you mean?'

Lili eyed him through narrowed eyes. Didn't he know the woman was crazy about him? If he didn't he must be blind.

He laughed softly when she made no reply. It annoyed Lili intensely.

'What are you laughing at?'

'You. You are aching to know about my wife and my relationship with Christina.'

'I am not! If I were I would ask you outright, and as I didn't that shows you I'm not in the least bit interested.' To prove it she walked out to the courtyard and started to gather up the dirty wine glasses, rather a lot of them. To her disconcertment Vittorio followed her.

'Christina and I are not lovers——'

'I didn't think you were——'

'I think you did,' Vittorio insisted. 'Hence the remark about Christina being disappointed that I don't believe in divorce.' He sat down under the vine to watch her clearing up. 'She is a distant cousin, many times removed, I think. I employ her to look after my home and my son when I am not able to.'

'You really didn't have to tell me that,' she said quietly. She felt quite ashamed for thinking there was something between them. She'd been mistaken about his feelings but she was sure she wasn't mistaken about Christina's. Perhaps he hadn't seen it because he wasn't looking for it.

'But I did. I have the feeling it is something between us that should be got rid of.'

Lili's hands tightened round the neck of the half-empty wine bottle. 'You have a lot of odd feelings, Vittorio,' she breathed wearily. 'I might have admitted, under duress, I must say, that I thought you attractive, but it doesn't mean I want an affair with you.'

He was smiling as he said, 'That is the first time you have used my Christian name; does that mean that you are softening towards me?'

'It probably means I'm going "soft" in the head.'

'And you mentioned affair once again and I didn't, so that must feature in your thoughts a lot.'

She hated the way he smiled slickly when he trapped her. 'I read minds,' Lili snapped irritably, 'though I don't have to delve too deeply into yours. You might as well have your intentions tattooed on your forehead or somewhere else that dominates your life!'

He laughed and reached for her wrist as she went to pick up the tray. 'Sit down; I want to enjoy you.'

'And I want to clear away!'

'And I don't want you to. There is more I have to tell you.'

Lili slumped into the seat across from him, knowing she shouldn't let him bamboozle her so easily, but it was hot and she was—curious.

'I'm all ears,' she urged, 'but remember one thing—nothing you will say will change my mind about you or make me change my mind about selling this house.'

He raised a positive brow. 'It isn't my intention to change your mind about how you feel about me; I'm quite happy with the way things are progressing between us. As for the house, you can go which way you like and it won't change *my* mind. It stays in your possession, not anyone else's.'

'We'll see about that,' Lili said tightly. 'Now where were we? Weren't you about to tell me more about let's-kick-cats-today Christina?'

He smiled knowingly. 'I think you know enough. I've told you we are not lovers; aren't you satisfied with that?'

'Satisfied isn't the word, uninterested is.'

'You lie very sweetly but unconvincingly. Let me stress that Christina is employed by me and is definitely not potential wife material.'

Lili wondered if Christina knew that. 'Are...are you looking for a wife?' Lili asked hesitantly, failing to ask the question that came before that one—what happened to the first wife?

'I want love, as most people want it, but my emotional demands are high.'

'And what are the emotions you demand?' She wondered why she was asking this as if she was actually interested. Trouble was she was, she resigned hopelessly—interested and curious.

'Passion, romance, honesty, sincerity...a few dozen more besides.'

Lili smiled and shook her head. 'I think you demand too much. I don't think a woman with that lot exists.'

Certainly not Christina, she thought ruefully, not able to get the picture of her at the airport out of her mind. And little Carlo—the boy had said he hated her. She shrugged away that notion as being fantasy; small boys often said things they didn't mean. Anyway, none of this conjecture was any of her business, but all the same she couldn't help feeling a deep sympathy for all concerned. All except Vittorio; he didn't need her sympathy.

Lili stood up to take the tray inside the house. Vittorio stood up too. 'Don't you want to hear what else I have to say to you?'

'I know enough about you and Christina now to get the picture.'

'I didn't mean Christina. I wanted to tell you about my wife.'

Slowly Lili lowered the tray back to the table. She did and didn't want to know and also wondered why Vittorio wanted to tell her. Surprisingly she felt nervous, sort of wobbly inside.

'She's dead,' Vittorio told her very unemotionally. 'She died when Carlo was four months old.'

Lili paled and her heart pounded dully. 'I'm...I'm sorry,' she uttered ineffectually. Though his voice had been cold when he'd told her that, she saw the pain in his eyes and knew what Stefano must have meant. Vittorio Rossi's wife might not be in evidence but she was very much with him, even in death.

'You loved her very much, didn't you?' Lili spoke shakily.

He smiled but not as if recalling some great happiness. 'At one time she was my sun and my moon, then she became my hell.' Unexpectedly he leaned forward and lifted Lili's chin and caressed his thumb along her jawline. 'She was beautiful and at times could be amusing. She was English, like you. She lit my life for a short time and gave me my son and then in her death she gave me a life sentence to live with.'

His fingers still caressed her chin, the smooth, tantalising gesture racing her senses with confusion. He still loved his wife and yet he could be so sensuous to her. Then he shocked her deeply by pulling her into his arms.

This kiss superseded all others; hot and passionate, it panicked Lili, and in that panic she was unable to move, but her mind raced on in a fever. Every time he touched her it was for a reason. Firstly to try and influence her about the sale of the house, and now...

She wrenched her mouth from his, her hands coming up to push at his chest. Her lips were white as she spoke angrily. 'Don't do that! I'm not your wife——'

His hands bit into her shoulders and she saw a deep anger in his eyes. 'I didn't think for a minute you were——'

'You did!' Lili stormed. 'You were talking about her and still loving her and I...I was just here.'

His anger turned to amusement, so quickly that he stunned her into silence and immobility. 'So, *cara*, you believe that, do you? How very wrong you are. When I make love to you I won't be thinking of my wife, I assure you.'

'*When* you make love to me?' Lili cried incredulously, her heart pounding recklessly at the thought. 'When isn't a consideration, nor is if—a definite no is more like it.'

That irritating smile again. His hands rubbed her shoulders gently and his voice was soft and persuasive. 'I want you very much, *cara*. I want Lili Mayer, not my treacherous wife. It's why I told you—to clear the air between us. When we make love I want nothing between us but a mist of sensuous moisture.' His dark eyes held hers to intensify what he had said and then his mouth lowered to hers again, parting her lips, sealing the suggestion with the surety of his mouth.

Lili didn't fight or protest but swam in that milky void of indecision. He was offering her the freedom to love him. As the kiss deepened and his arms locked around her, drawing her ever deeper into that heady power he exuded, she didn't know if she would ever have the courage to take that freedom.

He drew back from her at last and she read the deep desire in his eyes and knew that temptation was within biting distance. She could sink her teeth into it, for pleasure and satisfaction, for as long as it took for a holiday romance to flare and die. But that was the problem. The flame might not die and she might burn in hell as he had when that mysterious treacherous wife of his had died. Now she knew how very wrong she had been in thinking passion and excitement were all. Passion and excitement were dangerous and painful and the likes of dull, boring Simeon seemed a far safer option.

He caressed her damp hair from her forehead and smiled at the confusion dancing in her eyes.

'I think in the circumstances of this afternoon that it would be wiser if we altered the dinner arrangement for tonight...' Lili's heart raced her agreement, and yet disappointment at not seeing him this evening also vied for her pulse-rate. Very confusing. 'Instead I will come to you,' he added suggestively.

Lili opened her mouth to protest but he covered it with his soft, warm mouth in a fleeting kiss before turning away from her. He'd reached the opening to the outer courtyard and Lili hadn't moved. He turned and smiled and added, 'I will be alone, but you know that, don't you?'

He didn't expect an answer and Lili didn't give one; she just watched nervously as he walked through the opening and away into the vineyards. He'd be back at nightfall, expecting dinner and...

Lili trembled and picked up the tray and the glasses rattled her to her senses. She didn't have to do anything she didn't want to—if only she knew what that was!

CHAPTER FIVE

LILI dressed carefully. To go overboard would encourage him, to dress casually would show indifference. Lili sank to the edge of the bed in her spicy flame skirt and matching crinkly cotton blouse. But really there was no choice. This was the best she had brought, not expecting any more than lounging around her father's villa and soaking up some sun and local colour.

But Vittorio Rossi had been here when she had arrived and with very little effort he seemed to have changed her life, though she wasn't sure how or why. She just felt different. She thought about him most of the time, most of the time unwillingly. She stood up again and looked at herself in the mirror on the wall. She preferred indifference to encouragement, and perhaps she had achieved that with only a blush of lipstick and a few unnecessary strokes of mascara. Her hair had already taken the sun and there were streaks of gold and red among the tawny brown, and her skin glowed with a hint of bronze; there was nothing she could do to play down her attractiveness. She smiled to herself. She felt good and she looked good, and if she had packed the crown jewels she would have worn them tonight, so who was she kidding about indifference?

'Something smells delicious.'

Lili's heart pitched nervously at the sight of him when he walked into the long room. He was casually dressed, she was glad to see, but there was casual and casual. How could someone be casually elegant, casually sophisticated? Vittorio Rossi achieved it in black trousers and a terracotta-coloured silk shirt that looked weighty yet cool in the heat of the evening.

'I didn't know what to cook but thought pasta was a safe bet,' she told him as he took a bottle of Chianti from the wine-rack and proceeded to open it. He did it as if it was the most natural thing in the world to do, as if they lived together, as if they knew each other so well and were perfectly at ease in each other's company. But for Lili that was far from the truth. Her stomach was knotted inside her as she stirred the ricotta and ham sauce for the fettuccine, and it was nothing to do with her culinary skills.

'My favourite food, but then anything you cook for me would be my favourite.'

Lili smiled. 'There's no need to be sarcastic.'

'Was I being?'

'You know you were.'

'You know me well already.' He smiled as he poured two glasses of wine. Lili doubted that. Too many questions lay unanswered and he was as much a mystery now as when first they had met. All she knew for sure now was that he had had a wife whom he'd loved very much and he wasn't coping with her death very well.

'I'm sorry it's nothing more original than pasta, but you did rather spring this on me by inviting yourself to dinner.'

'If I hadn't invited myself, would you have invited me?'

'No.'

'But you accepted my dinner invitation.'

'Because Carlo would have been disappointed if I hadn't.' That wasn't the whole reason; the rest was that she had been madly curious to see how he lived.

'He's disappointed I wouldn't allow him to come tonight.'

And Lili bet Christina was choking on feathers too. 'You should have brought him,' Lili suggested. She poured the aromatic sauce over the pasta and slid it into the oven before she looked at him. He hadn't said a word to her last comment and when she saw the look in his eyes she knew why.

'It would have been safer if I had, wouldn't it?' he asked her throatily as their eyes met, and she realised that was what he had been waiting for— her eyes meeting his.

Lili didn't answer because there was no answer. She didn't really know what she expected out of the evening or even wanted. She watched him raise his wine glass to his lips, the lips that had touched her heart and senses and weighed her down with confusion and uncertainty. She felt the potency of the wine though she hadn't raised it to her lips yet. It was almost as if, if she did it now, as he tasted his wine, it would be a gesture of commitment that they both would understand without a word being spoken. The meal and the wine and the heat of the night would lead them to what had been on her mind since she had first met this man. Desire.

Lili bit her lip and lifted her glass from the work surface where he had left it for her. There, it was

out—the emotion she had tried to quash and tread
to the bottom of the emotion pit. He had excited
her desire to the rim where it hovered, tempting her
down. No man had ever made her feel this way
before. This bubbling inside, this fire and heat and
fear. But desire wasn't enough. Desire should go
hand in hand with love, and she didn't know much
about either and life was very confusing.

She swallowed some of the wine but the commitment wasn't made. There was too much fear of
being hurt, too much of a contest with a deceased
wife and too much uncertainty in her heart.

'I'm not going to bed with you, Vittorio,' she
said softly.

Her openness momentarily surprised him, for he
took a while to say, 'You don't sound very convinced of that.'

She looked at him bravely and answered him
honestly. 'I'm not.' He raised a surprised brow at
that and she smiled. 'It would be very easy to let
the night and the wine and you go to my head,' she
murmured, 'but tomorrow is always there.'

'And what will tomorrow bring for you if we
make love tonight?'

'Many things,' she answered. 'I've no doubt you
would be a charismatic lover but I can't forget the
hostility you showed me when I arrived. Your
opinion of me has changed pretty drastically—too
drastically to be genuine.'

'You believe I still have the motive for desire?'
he asked darkly, that tiny pulse at his jawline
straining to hold back his anger.

Lili shrugged and leaned back against the sink.
'I can't see what else it could be.' She thought there

might be another reason for him wanting her. She was English, like his wife, and might remind him of her, and that thought disturbed her enough to know that she wouldn't allow herself to be tempted tonight.

'Then I was mistaken about your emotions; they are only skin-deep.'

'They can't be anything else at the moment,' Lili told him quietly. 'Yours neither. We don't know each other.'

'And what better way to get to know each other than making love?' he suggested, the tense pulse easing.

Lili smiled and sipped her wine. 'That was an incredibly chauvinistic remark to make. In our country we do things differently. We get to know each other first and then we fall in love and then we make love.'

'That sounds very boring.' He was smiling now and Lili felt the tension ease from her limbs because he wasn't taking this conversation seriously. 'There is no thrill then, no excitement, and the fire in the loins is already cooling.'

Lili couldn't help laughing. 'So you think it more exciting to make love to a stranger than to someone you have grown to know and love?'

'I think there is a place for both in our lives.'

'That sounds very promiscuous.'

'I didn't mean it to be. I got to know and love my wife before I married her and our love-life was a great disappointment. She didn't fire me . . .'

'I don't think I want to hear this.' Lili squirmed inside. The mention of his wife made her feel very odd and she was shocked too that he could make such a personal admission. But this man didn't run true to form and he certainly wasn't dull and boring.

Vittorio refilled his wine glass and said openly, 'Does the thought of me making love to my wife make you feel so very uncomfortable?'

Heat rose to her cheeks because that was just it—she did feel uncomfortable and it wasn't because of modesty but something else: jealousy. She gripped her glass fiercely in her hand. Yes, jealousy thrust through her at the thought of him making love to his wife. And it had been jealousy that had prickled her against Christina. The discovery was so disturbing that she gulped a huge mouthful of wine and swallowed it before it touched the sides.

'It isn't the thought that bothers me,' Lili braved at last, 'it's the whole implication of what you are saying. You loved your wife—you said she was your sun and your moon—and yet your marriage didn't work, and it doesn't sound as if you had much of a love-life. There was something very wrong somewhere.'

'Indeed there was. She didn't love me so she made no effort to please me. I discovered that very soon into the marriage.'

She hadn't loved him? How could a woman marry a man and not love him, especially if that man was Vittorio Rossi? Heat invaded Lili's skin. She found him attractive but love was something else, surely?

'Some people say you don't have to be in love to enjoy *making* love,' she retorted brittly.

He shook his head and laughed softly. 'Some people,' he echoed. 'But you, Lili, do you believe that?'

Lili laughed tremulously. She could so easily fall into a trap here if she wasn't careful. 'I've never been in love,' was all she was prepared to give away.

'So you haven't made love?' Vittorio's eyes were dancing as if the question was a joke.

The wine had partly numbed Lili and she was able to smile secretly, and that *was* a joke. 'That would be telling, wouldn't it?'

He smiled. 'I think I get the picture. You want love *and* sex.'

'Yes, of course, and that is where women differ from men. Women usually want the whole package, men just want the gift-wrapping.'

'I agree the sexes differ, but that is only a generalisation. There are always exceptions to the rule.'

'Are you one?' she asked daringly. She'd never spoken to a man so openly about such a subject before.

'I think I must be. I have made love to women since my wife died but...' He shrugged. 'But maybe I am an exception to the rule.'

Lili turned to the oven. And those women hadn't satisfied him. Probably because he was chasing a dream, a substitute for the wife he loved so much.

'Let's eat before my pasta spoils,' she suggested flatly.

They carried the food outside to the rustic table under the vine. It was very hot and there wasn't a breath of air to stir the heat away. Lili lit a candle in the stillness while Vittorio dished up the food. She'd made a salad of oranges and tomatoes to go with the pasta.

Vittorio poured more wine as they ate.

'This tastes as good as it smells,' Vittorio said.

'I like cooking,' Lili told him, wishing she had
more occasions like this in her life to practise her
skills. It was heady stuff eating and drinking wine
out in the open. Maybe that was why the
Mediterranean people were supposedly so romantic
and hot-blooded. Lili wondered if they really were.
She had only Vittorio to go by and he...

'What are you thinking?'

Lili laughed into her wine. If only he knew. 'I
couldn't possibly tell you.'

'Why?'

'Because I'm almost sure you would challenge
me to prove a point.'

'That sounds very interesting so consider the
challenge thrown anyway.'

Lili smiled across the candle flame. 'Tell me
about Emilia.'

Vittorio frowned. 'Has she anything to do with
what you were just thinking?'

'No, I wanted to change the subject but I also
want to know about her too.'

'What *were* you thinking about just now?'
Vittorio insisted. 'I'd much rather talk about that
than Emilia. Emilia is past and I want the present.'

'I might not have been thinking about anything
in the present,' Lili teased.

'I'd still like to know.'

Lili cradled her wine glass in her fingers and
smiled. 'All right, I'll be absolutely truthful with
you and tell you what I was thinking on condition
that when I've said it you'll tell me about Emilia
and my father.'

Vittorio nodded. 'OK, it's a deal.'

Lili took a deep breath. 'I was thinking how nice all this is, eating and drinking outside in this lovely courtyard. Just the sound of the cicadas, the scent of herbs and the warmth all around you.'

'The stars above and the moon silvering the vines on the hillside,' Vittorio murmured.

Lili tilted her head and gazed across the table at him. 'So it's true.'

'What is?' Vittorio asked softly.

'That the sun warms the blood of the Mediterranean people.'

'And turns their blood to spitting fire.'

Lili laughed lightly. 'Now you've spoilt it. There was I, thinking you were so very romantic to say that about the moon and the vines and now you are talking of something quite different.'

'Passion, you mean? It can be romantic or it can be something completely different, depending what you want out of life.'

'And what do you want out of life, Vittorio?'

He didn't answer but pushed his plate away and pulled the fruit bowl towards him. He took a damp peach from the bowl and split it open with his thumbs. Lili watched enthralled as he raised the fruit to his lips and sucked the flesh from the skin. The movement was so erotic and suggestive that she wondered if he had done it for her benefit or if it just came naturally to him. He was a very sexy man, she realised with a rush of hot blood to her head. She smiled inwardly. Did she too have that sort of passion within her, waiting for the right man to release it?

'I want what Hugo and Emilia had,' he said at last, placing the remains of the ravaged peach down on his plate.

'And ... and what did they have?' She thought she knew but wanted to hear it from him.

'A love like that,' he murmured, locking his dark, broody eyes into hers.

Lili leaned forward. 'And what was that love like?'

He smiled wryly. 'The very best—total, earth-stopping, life-consuming, every damned cliché you care to mention.'

'You saw it all, didn't you?' Lili uttered hoarsely, wishing she had seen it too.

He nodded. 'And was jealous of it. Not in a spiteful self-destructive way but just a deep, deep envy.'

Oh, how she understood. Wasn't it what everyone sought in life, a love that was total?

'It's strange to hear a man make such an admission,' Lili said heavily. 'I've always thought men to be so calculating where love is concerned.'

'You obviously haven't met the right sort of men.'

Lili nodded her agreement. It had taken this trip out to Tuscany for her to realise that men like Vittorio Rossi existed, and yet he had a bitter streak to him, a cool arrogance and even a fair slice of cruelty which she supposed all went to make up his passion. His passion. She knew in that moment that she wanted it.

'Would you like some coffee?' she breathed, breaking the spell.

'Yes, but I insist on making it.' He stood up and gazed down at her and there was something dark and unfathomable in that look.

'Thank you. I'll clear the table.'

Vittorio went back into the house and Lili sat for a while, listening to the night sounds, breathing the warm, musky air. She wanted Vittorio Rossi. The thought repeated itself in her head till she felt dizzy with it. And she could have what she wanted. She closed her eyes momentarily and was lost in that fantasy but then realism hit her. She too wanted what her father and his mistress had had—a love that was total; but where did it begin and how did you recognise it when you were faced with it, and was Vittorio Rossi the man to answer all her inner doubts?

Lili piled up the plates and carried them through to the kitchen. Vittorio was taking his time with the coffee.

He was by the cooker waiting for the water to boil and looked up as she walked into the room. At the same time the oil lamp above the cooker dimmed and started to smoke. Vittorio reached up and lowered the wick.

'The oil has run out.'

'I'll get the candle from outside,' Lili said, turning to grope her way out of the kitchen.

Her wrist was caught and suddenly she was in his arms, his breath hot on her cheek as he feverishly sought her mouth. His lips on hers were hard and impassioned and Lili wondered where she had got the impression that the man was romantic. The kiss frightened her with its ferocity and she tried to pull away, but he held her fast.

'You're hurting me.'

His body relaxed but not enough for her to move out of his reach. 'I'm sorry,' he murmured and then his mouth sought hers once again and this time there was softness and a silent plea for forgiveness.

Instead of the dizzy submission she had fantasised about outside in the courtyard there was a rush of doubt and fear in Lili's heart. She wanted him and he wanted her but something was very wrong.

'I can't,' she husked, pushing him away.

She heard his soft laughter as she groped her way out to the laundry-room. The candle on the table lit the rest of the way and she stumbled towards it, but before she could lift it he was behind her, swinging her round into his arms.

'Because you want to hear words of love before giving yourself to me?'

'No,' Lili blurted, 'not that... I mean...' Oh, yes, just that. She wanted to love and be loved and not used.

'I know what you mean.' Suddenly his voice held no softness. 'You are no different. You calculate just like all females. You tempt and tease and then grind your heels in...'

Shocked, Lili protested, 'Where have you been for the last hundred years? I'm not a tease and I'm not grinding my heels in. I just want to be treated like a human being!'

He let her go as if she were carrying a deadly virus. Lili lifted her hands and touched his arms because she felt she had been harsh. 'Look, Vittorio Rossi,' she said quietly. 'I want everything out of life you want. I want passion and excitement, I want what my father and Emilia had; what I don't want is to make a mistake.'

'The way your father did with his first marriage?' His hands came up to clench her arms.

That was partly the reason, she realised suddenly; maybe it was all of the reason, maybe that was why she was seeking something that very probably was a myth-perfection. 'And like you with your first marriage,' she said bravely. 'Somehow you got yourself into a situation that ended in a marriage that shouldn't have taken place...' He tightened his grip on her and she knew she had struck home. 'I'm sorry; that's not my business but yours. What I'm trying to say is I don't want to be used and...and I feel you are using me...'

He laughed softly in the balmy night air. 'And where have you been for the last hundred years, Lili Mayer? Women are equally skilled at using men. You are using me now.'

She was surprised by that. 'Oh, and how do you work that out?'

'You want stroking too, but on your terms. You are skilled with your words, trying to make me admit to more than I'm prepared to at the moment. You say you don't want to make a mistake. It could be a mistake to hold back your passion and your desire. How will you ever taste life unless you take some risks?'

'And that risk would take the form of making love to you, would it?' she smarted back at him.

'Why not?' he laughed. He lowered his mouth to hers but this time there was a subtle difference. This wasn't serious, this was a tease, a temptation, and very probably a punishment for her perversity.

But there was more than just his lips brushing hers. His hand came up and smoothed so tenderly over her breast that she nearly cried out. His thumb teased over her nipple and the explosion of her senses was immediate and overpowering, the need so strong that it crazed her mind. He eased slightly away from her and though her eyes were tightly shut she sensed he was gazing down at her.

The soft rhythm of his caress of her breast didn't ease up. She heard the deep, laboured breath rumble in his chest and felt the rise in the heat from his body. Slowly she raised her lashes to look up at him.

There was triumph in the gleam in his eye, desire too, deep, deep desire, but the control in that glint of iron in his eyes was terrifying. In fear Lili went to pull away from him, but that steely determination that he wasn't going to be used either spurred him to grip her even tighter against him.

'I can play games too, *cara*.' His lips brushed hers again, his hands skimmed down to her hips and he ground her hard against his arousal. 'I can't disguise that,' he gravelled at her throat, 'but I can control what I do with it. If you want to play games I'm a willing opponent. I just hope you know how not to play dirty and how to be an honourable loser.'

He drew back from her, sharply, abruptly, his withdrawal so shockingly effective that she felt as if he had physically withdrawn from deep inside her.

'Sleep well, if you can,' he drawled silkily and walked away from her, across the courtyard to the door in the wall and the desolate vineyards beyond.

Lili stood for a very long time in the hot courtyard after he had left. The pain inside her was real—an ache of loss, an ache of sheer frustration.

Vittorio Rossi had done what no man had ever done before. He had excited her, filled her with a desire that demanded satisfaction and then ... and then just walked away, controlling *his* desire with an abruptness she found terrifying in its cold calculation.

Lili cleared away by candle-light, took herself up to bed by candle-light and lay in the stuffy night watching the shadows thrown by candle-light. It was hard to rationalise her feelings. She had some for that arrogant man, but he was complex and he was also different from any other man she had met. Love by difference, she mused. A life with him would be stimulating, to say the least.

Lili leaned up and blew out the candle and slumped back against her pillow with a thin smile on her face. But he wasn't offering her a life or a love, just a portion of his time, seduction time. He wanted to make love to her and disposable passion was probably the ruling force; once he got what he wanted he would cast her aside. He said he wanted what her father and Emilia had had, but Lili couldn't imagine him ever finding it. At least it was something they both had in common: a deep longing for a love that was total.

Lili turned her face into the pillow and swallowed hard. It must have been very special and Vittorio had witnessed it all. She wished with all her heart that she had.

*   *   *

'Oil for the lamps,' Vittorio said the next morning, placing a canister down by the side of the scrubbing-sink.

Lili was hot and exhausted, pummelling away at the harsh stone.

'Did Emilia do this every day? Some love and devotion,' she grated ruefully. She scooped up an armful of sopping T-shirts and plopped them into a basket to take outside. Vittorio stooped down and picked it up for her. They both went outside to the courtyard.

'A woman came up from the village every day. Emilia didn't do all this.'

'And there was I thinking that love was something special.'

'Would you do this for the man you loved?' Vittorio asked her, handing her a T-shirt to hang over the line she had rigged up from the fig tree.

'No way. I can think of better things to do with my time than slave over a stone sink.'

'Ah, you are this new breed of women who puts a career before a home life.'

'This isn't a home life, Vittorio, this is pure un-adulterated drudgery, and I bet that Christina doesn't do this every day.'

'You're right, she doesn't,' Vittorio laughed.

Lili laughed with him, her heart straining very hard under her thin cotton top. He was so *nice* when he laughed.

'Thanks for the oil. How much do I owe you?' They were back in the kitchen, Lili reaching for her purse on the work surface.

Vittorio clamped his hand over her wrist. 'You know the only payment I want.'

Lili tried to control the tension in her wrist. 'Yes, I know,' she murmured, 'but I can't afford you.'

'The expense of your emotions?'

She levelled her eyes at his and answered very truthfully, 'Yes, exactly that. They are not to be bartered for like some cheap holiday souvenir. You did us both a favour by walking out as you did last night; if you had stayed we might have made love and I would have regretted it. It gave me time to think. I'm not going to be manipulated. I want to sell this house and go home...'

Vittorio's hand tightened on her wrist. 'I can stop you doing both,' he threatened darkly.

Lili narrowed her lips. 'You can't, Vittorio. The house is mine to sell——'

'The land it stands on isn't,' he interrupted very softly. A supercilious smile creased his mouth as Lili took that in.

Lili parted her lips to croak feebly, 'And precisely what is that supposed to mean?'

'That the house is yours and the land mine and no one in their right mind would buy a house that didn't have its own land under it.'

Lili's eyes widened in disbelief. 'But...but Stefano wants to buy it...he's a solicitor...he would know these things...he would know if the land didn't go with the house.' This was some sort of bluff. Vittorio Rossi couldn't have a claim on the land; he was trying to scare her.

'Bellini is a fool, Lili, a greedy fool. His talent lies with legislation, not property developement. He's seen others make a lot of money out of land deals and thought he would try the same. When

you see him, tell him to check his facts before
making silly offers that mean absolutely nothing.'

Slowly but determinedly Lili drew her wrist out
of his hand. Now she didn't doubt his words.
Vittorio had no reason to lie and she hadn't liked
Bellini, so could well believe these accusations.
'So...so the land is yours?' she uttered weakly.
Vittorio nodded his dark head. 'So...so I can't
sell?'

'You never could. I told you that.'

Oh, he'd told her a lot of things and led her to
believe a lot more. Funny, but she really didn't care
that she couldn't sell her father's house. In some
ways it was a relief to know she couldn't. She'd had
so many doubts since living among her father's and
Emilia's belongings. It would have broken her heart
to have parted with it, and especially to Bellini, who
would have rolled the place over, no doubt. So
Vittorio had no motive for desire as she had accused him, and yet still he wanted her. So why didn't
she feel some sort of elation at that?

She turned away, confused. 'You should have
told me sooner,' she said quietly.

'For what purpose?'

She swung back to him angrily. 'Because you just
should have done! You misled me. I wouldn't have
stayed if I'd have known.'

'Because you couldn't make a killing from your
father's estate?' he shot back bitterly.

'No! Not that!' Lili cried. 'Why do you make
me out to be such a mercenary bitch?'

'I don't think that, not now,' he growled back.
'But when you first arrived I had grounds enough
to think that way. You gave me no explanation for

why you didn't come to your father's funeral. What are you hiding?'

'You . . . you rat!' Lili cried, lifting her hand to take a swing at the side of his face. He caught her wrist, easily deflecting the blow. Lili didn't give up so easily. She wrenched her wrist from his fingers and spun away from him. 'Just get out and leave me alone!'

'You're mean when you're aroused, aren't you?' he grated darkly. 'I was beginning to think you were indeed your father's daughter but you're not. You are mercenary . . .'

'Just you stop there!' Lili cried, waving an indignant forefinger at him. 'Don't you say one more insulting word. I am not mercenary and I did not come here to make a killing on my father's estate. Yes . . . yes, I thought about selling, *thought* about it, but if I knew I had no chance anyway I would have left sooner, and not because of what you think but because it hurts being here . . .' She stifled a sob before it swelled. 'It hurts to know you know more about my father than I do, it hurts that your son called him grandfather, it damn well hurts knowing he had a love that the likes of you and me will never have . . .'

Vittorio reached for her then and Lili reeled away from him, her eyes scorching with unshed tears. 'Don't touch me,' she sobbed. 'Just you get out, Vittorio Rossi . . .'

He grasped her firmly by the shoulders. 'So why stay and pain yourself that way if it wasn't to sell this place?'

'I . . .' She didn't know; she honestly didn't know why she was still here. She *had* wanted to sell at first and then something odd had happened. The villa and its secrets had held her and . . . and him, of course. Damn him!

'Perhaps you knew all along that this land was mine. Perhaps Bellini isn't the fool I thought he was and perhaps the two of you together are conniving with *my* emotions to get me to agree to release it . . .'

Shocked and bruised by his verbal onslaught, she moved her mouth viciously. 'You are crazy, out of your mind. I knew nothing till you just threw it in my face, like all the other insults you throw at me . . .'

'So far it's all been fact. Dear God, but I was right about you from the very start—a woman who couldn't even be bothered to attend her father's funeral. Couldn't you spare the time? Couldn't you . . . ?'

Lili's arms shot up to knock his hands from her shoulders. His hands tightened but Lili was quicker and wrenched away from him with a sob of anguish and pain. Vittorio's hands grasped at her thin cotton shirt and as she swung away the fabric tore, ripping the tiny buttons down the front till the cotton hung free from her shoulders. Her skimpy shorts were hip-hugging and she wore no bra under her top but her hands didn't shoot to her naked breasts for protection. They shot to the deep purple scar that ran from her navel across her waist. The scar that had never faded because the operation had been so frenetic.

Hot tears ran down her face then as she glared at him staring at the ugly disfigurement.

'Pre-pretty, isn't it?' she sobbed wildly and then she wanted to hurt him as he had hurt her, to hurt him with the painful truth that she hoped would stab at his conscience and that cold heart of his. 'This is what stopped me attending my father's funeral, Vittorio Rossi. Fighting for my own life while his ebbed away. I didn't know he had died. Because of this,' she wept, stabbing at the scar, 'I didn't even know if I was alive myself. Are you satisfied now; are you quite happy with that now?'

CHAPTER SIX

LILI flew then, turned and ran across the long room and up the stairs to her bedroom. The door jarred against his foot as she tried to slam it.

'I told you to get out!'

'I didn't hear you!' He pushed her back into the room, back against the bed. 'Tell me about it.'

'What?' she gasped, clutching at the remains of her top, trying in vain to cover her breasts now.

His hand came up and tore the last shreds of it away from her skin. His eyes were glazed with an anger she didn't understand.

'Tell me about it. I want to hear what happened.'

'You don't believe me, do you?' Lili cried bitterly.

His eyes softened, his hand came forward and he touched the scar, smoothed his fingers delicately over the desensitised area. Lili flinched as she always did when anything came in contact with the purple weal. It wasn't painful any more, just held painful reminders for her.

'Don't do that,' she uttered weakly.

'What happened?' he asked softly, not letting up the smooth caress across her waist. 'I want to hear what happened.'

She lowered her eyes. 'Appendix, it burst...the doctor...the doctor didn't know...nearly left it too late...'

'Dear God,' Vittorio breathed raggedly. He pulled her towards him, circled his powerful arms around her and buried his face in her silken hair. 'Why the hell didn't you tell me?'

'Why should I?' Lili whispered roughly and then she started to sob gently against him because it brought it all back. The terrible pain, the panic at the hospital, the emergency operation to save her life and then weeks later when she came out of her nightmare the worst pain of all—being told that her father had died.

'Because it was the reason you couldn't come to your father's funeral and I have tortured you with my terrible accusations.'

'You didn't know...'

'I didn't give you a chance to explain.' He drew back from her to cup her face in his hands. 'I'm sorry for that, Lili, deeply sorry.'

He lowered his mouth to hers and for a moment she swam dizzily as the kiss deepened sensuously. Her tears and anguish and the brutality of their harsh argument were drowned in a rush of comfort and need. Her fingers curled into his hair, her mouth parted and every pulse stalled and froze in time as the kiss went beyond return. But one small pulse remained to beat dully. The 'doubt' pulse, the one that was never far away when she was with Vittorio Rossi.

Her mouth curled away from his and she breathed deeply before murmuring her refusal. She felt him tense, felt the sharp intake of breath in his chest against her breast.

'My punishment for last night?' he breathed savagely against her throat.

'No,' she harshed back, trying to put space and air between them with her clenched fists. 'But this is all wrong. *You* are all wrong. You want me for all the wrong reasons.'

He grasped those small fists and squeezed them tightly in his own and then with a swift jerk he tipped her back on the bed. In an instant he had straddled her, holding her hands above her head on the cotton coverlet. He towered over her, his eyes dark with anger. 'What reasons, for God's sake? What reasons do you think I have for wanting you?'

'You tell me!' Lili breathed equally rawly. 'One minute you are fighting me, the next you expect to make love to me. Why? To apologise for thinking the very worst of me? Because you feel sorry for me because of this scar? Because I remind you of your wife? Because you want what my father had? Well, my name isn't Emilia and yours isn't Hugo and...'

His teeth bared dangerously, half-smile, half-grimace, and for an instant Lili thought she had gone too far.

'I don't do that kind of thing as an apology, *cara*,' he breathed savagely, 'and I don't feel sorry for you. You think you know so much but you know so very little. We fight because of this.' His mouth swooped down to crush her mouth in a kiss that was more than passion and more than desire. It was death by kissing. Lili felt her life blood flow out of her with the fiery heat of that kiss. Her head swam and she understood why he tormented her and why she did much the same to him. It was the tension between them that provoked harsh words, harsh thoughts and the need to punish. The tension of need.

'Now do you understand?' he grated roughly after drawing back from her. 'I want you so much that I can't help what I say or do...'

'You can,' Lili blurted, still opposing him because knowing the reasons didn't help. 'It's called...called self-control...' Of which she had very little, she realised with mounting panic as he lowered his mouth to hers once again. The rise and fall of her emotions sickened her. She could want him and hate him and then want him more, all in the same swirling second.

She struggled and twisted under his grip. He released her hands but kept up the pressure on her mouth, and that was far more restricting than if he had bound her in chains. She didn't push him away, didn't struggle, because it was all too hopelessly late to retrieve her inhibitions. They were gone, willed away by his passionate persuasion. He wouldn't stop now and she didn't want him to; she knew her love made resistance impossible.

Satisfied she would struggle no more, he lowered his mouth tenderly to the scar on her waist. His tongue ran over it lightly, soothing away her tension and fear. Lili arched her back at the delicious tingling sensation and the cool relief that followed, and something deep inside her melted and fizzed, the very last protest gone in a *frisson* of defeat. She touched his shoulders tentatively and felt the heat through his shirt and she was afraid then that this was going to be a repeat of last night. The thought tensed her and she stiffened and tried to draw her knees up.

'No, *cara*,' he breathed deeply against her stomach. 'No tease this time. My heart cannot take the strain.' He raised himself up and looked down at her, one hand slowly, softly easing down her shorts.

The passion was in her heart in an instant; his passion was in his eyes as he watched his own hands caress the silk of her briefs. Lili turned her face to one side, unable to bear the fiery need in the blaze of his eyes.

'Don't be afraid,' he breathed reassuringly and the tenderness of his caress added to the reassurance.

She wasn't afraid, not any more. This was her choice, brought on by his sensual persuasion but nevertheless her own choice. Her hands and arms moved, slowly coming down to touch his hair, to smooth the black silkiness, to brush against his skin. His mouth fluttered kisses across her throat and she moaned submissively, moving against him, enticing him to go on.

He moved away from her to ease out of his clothes and Lili tried to help, but he laughed softly and gently pushed her hands away; then there was no more laughter as the urgency between them was accelerated by the bonding of their naked flesh. Feverishly they grasped at each other, mouthing half-kisses on warm skin, touching, smoothing, testing, tasting each other.

Vittorio's body was magnificent, firm and broad and warm. Lili ran her exploratory fingers over his smooth flesh and told him how beautiful he was.

Her softly murmured compliments surprised him. 'I'm the one supposed to say you are the beautiful one,' he said tenderly.

'Don't you like me speaking what's in my heart?' she whispered.

He tensed for a tiny second but long enough for Lili to be aware of it.

'I'm not used to it... I...' His voice trailed away and he brushed his lips hotly across her lips and Lili thought he had been about to speak of his wife but had stopped himself in time. But there had been women since his wife. Seven years was a long time, and surely someone had told him how beautiful he was? And he was beautiful. His skin was hard and yet silky, perfumed and warm, his hands devastatingly seductive. Every caress, every stroke drove her harder and more urgently to new peaks of awareness. She had never known the small of her back was a haven of such sweet pleasure. His thumbs pressed erotically at a point that had her sighing his name and clasping at his hips.

Vittorio rolled her gently over and put his mouth on the spot that had driven her to the edge of ecstasy and flicked his tongue tantalisingly over a nerve that had her moaning softly with pleasure and delight.

Unable to stand the sweet torture a second longer, she wriggled round to face him. He smiled down at her and his eyes were heavy with warmth. She smiled back and lifted her arms to enfold him in her love. She wanted to please him, to give him what no other woman had: her complete adoration. She had never done such a thing before, to any man. But suddenly it didn't seem to appear very difficult. Somehow the instincts were natural as if they had always been within her just waiting to be coaxed free by the right man.

Lili let go of all her doubts and inhibitions. Gently she touched him, smoothed the palms of her small hands down his broad chest, lower and lower, running the backs of her fingers over his taut stomach. The sweet pleasure was hers too, such sweet pleasure in discovering his sensitive zones. She smoothed her hands lower, growing confident, more daring, lower till she reached his magnificent arousal. Once again she felt that small tremor of tension as she touched him, as if he was afraid, and she closed her lips over his to reassure him that it was all right. Tentatively her fingers splayed around him, stroking his silken power, cupping it in both hands. He let out a long moan of pleasure and it excited Lili to do more.

'My God,' he breathed raggedly and then he drew his breath in harshly as Lili drew on him, running her tongue around the silken tip, pleasuring him to the fragile point of ecstasy and release. 'No, Lili!' he cried out suddenly, and then he pulled away from her, manoeuvring her under him and grasping her hips up to his.

He entered her immediately and she was ready for him. Soft and warm and pliant and not at all afraid. There was no pain and she knew why—because it was right and natural and something that was meant to hold no fear. She wrapped her arms around his neck and pressed her breasts against his heaving chest as the pressure inside her grew. His thrusts were masterful, spinning her towards a mysterious pleasure she had only ever dreamt about.

The sweet moisture between them was as he'd predicted—a scented love vapour that Lili kissed from his throat, running her tongue up to his parted lips, parting her own mouth to probe his inner sweetness. His response was all she ever wanted— a deep, deep moan of submissive desire, a deep, deep shudder of sheer ecstasy. The thought that she had such power over him excited her to move urgently with him, to respond to every thrust, to exult with him in the divine pleasure that surged through their heated bodies.

And then something magical broke between them, taking them both unawares and forcing cries to their lips in unison. It was a heat and a fire and an extra surge of power and Lili squeezed shut her eyes and arched blindly against him. Exquisitely the liquid fire coiled and tightened and then spun ever outwards, dispersing in a burst of power that shook through them both, leaving them trembling hard against each other, bonded together, bodily and spiritually.

They lay exhausted in each other's arms, hot and wet and drawing long breaths from the airless room. The midday sun was mercifully overhead and not penetrating the room, but the heat was nevertheless suffocating.

Neither could move, though. To separate would take too much effort.

At last Lili made some effort to move her head, to focus her misty eyes on Vittorio. He lay next to her with his eyes closed. For the first time she could appreciate the length and lushness of his eyelashes, the firm planes of his features, the softly defined line of his mouth. There wasn't an ounce of tension in his wonderful face or his body. She had drained it all away. Lili smiled and leaned her hot cheek against his shoulder. Lili Mayer had done that.

Somehow that person wasn't herself. But maybe it was the real Lili, one that had flowered under his touch and become her true self. She felt different. She was different. Love by difference.

She was content for a few minutes, lying next to him, listening to his soft breath, feeling his warmth hard against her own. She supposed he was asleep. She wanted to stay this way forever. Happily sated. Happily dreaming. She loved him...but... Tiny prickles of doubt stabbed at the base of her spine, just at the spot he had caressed and teased so lovingly a while ago. The prickles sharpened till they were a physical pain. Slowly she drew back from him, drawing herself back in mind and body. She loved him...but...but there was nothing on the wall to say he felt likewise.

Suddenly she was nervous—no, more than that, afraid, afraid that she had misinterpreted the whole affair. Oh, how she hated that word 'affair'.

Slowly she moved out of the bed, suddenly terrified that he would wake and see her naked. She bit her lip till it hurt. Naked; why was she so suddenly ashamed of that when he now knew every inch of her body? Shame, was that it? Was she honestly ashamed of their lovemaking?

She stood by the bed and gazed down at him, and felt an ache and a deep sorrow. There was no shame, you couldn't feel that way about something so beautiful and complete, but there was sorrow. She had given so much; she had given her heart. He had given too, but not his heart. That still lay with his wife, buried with her where no one could exhume it.

With a desperate shiver she grasped at her shorts, pulled them on and silently padded to the wardrobe for a clean top to replace the one he had shredded from her.

She took one more glance at him from the bedroom door. He hadn't moved, but when he did she would know how he felt about her. He would have to say something and she would know whether or not she had a chance in his life. And if she didn't, if there was no place for her? She couldn't face that yet; no, not yet.

She was in the kitchen when he eventually came down. She didn't know what to say or do so she said nothing but carried on attacking the stains in the porcelain sink with added vigour.

'Not very romantic,' he said, standing in the archway.

Lili turned then. 'What do you mean?' she said faintly.

He made no attempt to come closer. 'I expected to wake and find you warm and yielding next to me; instead I find you down here, cleaning the sink out.'

'Of course, I should have been lying next to you, just waiting for you to bless me with your consciousness...' Oh, God, why was she being this way, why was she saying such silly things?

'I expected you to be there,' he said darkly. 'We need to talk.'

Lili turned back to the sink. 'About what? Selling this house? What went wrong with your first marriage?'

As soon as it was out she knew she had made another mistake. She shouldn't be here doing this;

she should have stayed next to him in bed. By slipping away she had created a rift by mere separation. And now she had caused a bigger rift by mentioning his wife.

'I'm sorry,' she mumbled. 'I shouldn't have brought that up.'

'If you mean the apology, have the decency to deliver it to my face,' he clipped like a schoolteacher.

Embarrassed, Lili faced him again. She parted her lips to repeat the apology but it hovered on her lips at the sight of the pain and torture in his eyes. Did he miss his wife so very much?

'I'm sorry,' she said at last. 'I'm sorry for mentioning your wife but . . . but . . . if you want to talk about it . . .'

'I don't, I assure you,' he informed her icily. 'Our problems were beyond redemption.'

'But ours aren't,' Lili murmured softly. She wondered at her nerve for saying that. But they had a few problems, there was no escaping them, and if there was any future for them they had to be faced.

'If the relationship is fraught with problems from the start it doesn't stand much chance, Lili. I speak from experience, I assure you.'

Her heart went cold inside her. Did he mean their relationship, or his with his wife? She wanted to ask but couldn't. Her throat was dry and painful and for once she was at a loss for words. She swallowed hard and managed to muster a few.

'Well, there's nothing more to be said.' Her voice was iced to disguise her deep hurt. She groped for the tap and rinsed her hands furiously as if to wash him from her heart. She reached for a tea-towel and without giving him another look she walked out of the house to the courtyard.

'I'm sorry you feel so bitter about what happened——'

Lili swung to face him. 'Bitter?' she exclaimed, her hazel eyes so wide that they hurt. 'I'm not bitter, but you are for some unearthly reason. I *should* feel bitter; that's the normal thing for a woman to feel after she has been used——'

'Don't,' Vittorio pleaded, so effectively that all fight went from Lili's limbs, leaving her weak and useless. Her hand came up to knead her forehead. She'd made a mess of everything and there was no way out, and he wasn't helping a bit.

'Look, leave me alone. I want to be on my own. I don't want to talk, not about anything.'

He didn't speak, didn't argue, didn't even look sorry. But of course he had nothing to feel sorry about unless she wanted to torture herself with the thought that he might be feeling a smidgeon of remorse for using her as a reminder of the wife he had loved and lost.

Bleakly she watched him cross the shady courtyard to the door that led to the vineyards, and then he was gone. Out of her life? she wondered, and closed her eyes in despair. Please not that, she silently prayed; don't let it end like this.

'So how long do you need to cool your heels?' Lili spoke into the vineyards two days later. There was no answer because there was no one there. She had convinced herself that this was all his fault and that when he came to his senses he would realise he had been unjust. And he had, but she really wasn't sure why or how. They had made love and then it had all gone wrong and for no real apparent reason.

Lili turned back to the group of cats crowded round the bowls she had put down for them. Love was strange and unreasonable and not as easy as people imagined. Animals didn't suffer in such a way.

The pregnant tabby was lethargic today, sprawled in the cardboard box Vittorio Rossi had been so scathing about.

Lili glanced up into the sky. There were clouds above, the atmosphere was thick and humid and she felt a summer storm approaching; she welcomed it. Storms sometimes had the effect of snapping people's tension. Would Vittorio snap out of his tension and come to her?

Lili had put the box on its side, protected by a clump of scented oleanders against the wall, and now she covered it with a sheet of polythene she had found in the laundry-room. If it rained the tabby would be dry. She was near her time, Lili sensed.

The first droplets of rain came late in the afternoon; by nightfall the storm was at full throttle and Lili knew that time was running out for her and Vittorio. She'd practised what she would say to him when he came but now it looked as if he never would.

Lili showered away the oppressive heat and wrapped herself in her cotton bathrobe. She lit a bundle of candles and stood them in the empty grate to cheer the dismal night and curled on the sofa to read, but the light was too bad and she couldn't be bothered to light the oil lamp. She lay and stared at the beamed ceiling. Should she go to him, climb through that vineyard to his house in the hills, say what she wanted to say—that she loved him and wanted his heart to be free to love her? But no, she could never do that. He was still steeped in the past, regretting the death of his wife, wishing he could find what Hugo and Emilia had.

'Yes, I am crazy,' Lili muttered, getting to her feet, 'crazy to want to get involved in his complicated emotional life when he obviously doesn't want to be in mine...'

Her heart lurched as she heard a sound outside. It somersaulted at the thought that it might be Vittorio. She flung open the front door but there was nothing but wet and more wet. She slammed the door shut and, taking a candle in a saucer, she went to the kitchen to make herself a drink but tensed again as she heard a scraping sound come from the courtyard.

There was fear now, not hope. Every night a group of village men passed the villa on their way to the vineyards for their walk and their gossip, and Lili often waved. Had one of them taken that gesture of friendliness the wrong way? Her bones froze.

Now she heard a small cry...the miaow of a cat? Lili relaxed. The tabby giving birth. She reached up, lit the oil lamp and unhooked it, and went to the laundry-room door. It was too wet to go right outside but she knew the cat was dry and warm and best left alone anyway. She was shutting the door when she heard a small whimper.

It came from the rustic table. Fearlessly Lili
hobbled across the courtyard in her bare feet,
soaked to the skin before she had gone two steps.

'Carlo!' Lili cried. 'What on earth...?' She
reached down for him but he shrank away from
her.

'Get out from under there, Carlo!' There was no
coaxing him out with soft words, so Lili let rip. She
reached under the table and hauled him out by his
collar. 'Get inside the house before you drown.'

He stumbled ahead of her, soaked to the skin
like her. They stood and faced each other in the
kitchen, both dripping, both slightly shaking.

'Are...are you cross with me?' Carlo uttered.

'Furious!' Lili cried. 'What on earth are you
doing here?' She didn't wait for his answer but
snatched a clean towel from the basket in the
laundry-room and tousled his dripping hair dry.

'Ouch, that hurts.'

Lili slowed the pace then cried out when she saw
the blood on the towel.

'Oh, Carlo, you've cut yourself.'

'I fell, slipped in the mud; I was frightened.'

Lili knelt down on the stone floor and swaddled
him like a baby and held him hard against her. Her
fury at seeing him had been so terribly selfish. Her
first thought had been that the child had run away
and soon Vittorio would be here and making all
sorts of bitter accusations, probably suggesting she
had enticed him away to get his attention. Oh, she
was paranoid about that damned man, and this
poor child was injured.

Fifteen minutes later she had showered him,
dressed the graze on his forehead, wrapped him in

a cotton blanket and tucked him up on the sofa. She called out from the kitchen as she made him a warm milky drink. 'Your *papà* will be here in a minute, Carlo; do you feel like telling me what all this is about?' She added a spoonful of honey to the milk and stirred it as she went back to the sitting-room.

'I wanted to see the kittens, to see if they were born,' Carlo volunteered, so softly that Lili was immediately suspicious.

'In the middle of the night, in the pouring rain?'

Carlo's huge brown eyes locked into hers for a second as he reached for the drink and then he hastily averted them.

'Carlo,' Lili insisted, more gently now because she sensed the boy was troubled. 'Please tell me what's wrong.' Had there been a family row? Perhaps Vittorio had chastised him for something and he had run away. 'Well, if you're not going to talk we'll just wait for your father to come and collect you——'

'Papà won't come,' Carlo blurted quickly.

'Of course he will.' She bit her lip. But perhaps he wouldn't. Perhaps he hated her so much now that he'd send Christina instead. 'He'll come just as soon as he discovers you're missing.'

'He won't know I'm here.'

Lili hadn't considered that. 'That's a point,' she murmured worriedly. 'But he'll check here first——'

'He won't!' Carlo insisted so emphatically that Lili frowned.

'Nothing for it but to drive you back my-self, then.'

'You can't. The road will be out; it always washes away in the rain.'

Lili sighed. She wasn't getting very far. 'It will have to be the bell, then——'

'No...not the bell. I don't like the bell; Nonna rang the bell...' Suddenly Carlo burst into tears, spilling his milk as he tried to cover his face.

Lili scooped the mug out of his hands, put it on the floor and drew the weeping child into her arms. For some reason the bell had bad connotations for him.

'It's all right, Carlo,' she soothed quietly. 'I won't ring the bell. We'll just wait for your *papà*——'

'He...he won't come...he's gone away!' the boy burst out angrily. 'He always goes away... I hate it——'

'Carlo!' Lili cried, shocked and holding him at arm's length by his small, shaking shoulders. 'Did he go out and leave you? Surely not. He wouldn't do that. 'What about Christina? Where's Christina?' Dear God, but surely the child hadn't been left alone in the house on a night such as this— or any night, come to that?

'Papà is away...on business...and I'm glad!' he suddenly spurted vehemently, fiercely rubbing his wet nose with the back of his hand. 'He was cross all the time and shouted at everybody and he made Christina cry. Then he went away and then...then tonight...Christina made me go to bed early and...and the storm came and I was frightened and when I got up she had gone——'

'Left? Left the house?' Lili cried in disbelief, her eyes so wide that they matched the size of Carlo's own huge, moist pools.

'Sometimes she goes out when Papà isn't home. She leaves me and says I mustn't tell and she goes to drink in the village——'

Shock waves crashed through Lili's body as she gathered the boy back into her arms. 'No more, Carlo,' Lili whispered, brushing her mouth across his feverish brow. 'I don't need to hear any more.'

Lili was shocked and so angry that she hurt with it, but she hid it all under a cloak of concern for the boy. Ten minutes later he was settled in Hugo and Emilia's bed, his eyelids already drooping with fatigue as Lili tucked the sheet up under his chin.

When she was sure he was soundly asleep she blew out the candle and went downstairs and sat on the sofa with her head in her hands. How could Vittorio allow this to happen to his son? She was sure he loved him—no man could be that heartless—but already the boy was at boarding-school and when he was home he was in the despicable hands of that awful Christina.

She sighed deeply. It was a sad fact of life that it was none of her business, but when either Christina or Vittorio came to collect Carlo she would have her say—oh, boy, would she have her say!

CHAPTER SEVEN

LILI heard movement downstairs in the early hours of the morning. She got up quickly, slid into her cotton robe, which was quite dry now, lit a candle and hurried to her father's bedroom. Carlo was still sleeping peacefully and there was only one person with access to the villa.

With relief she ran down the stone stairs. She'd rather give Vittorio a dressing-down than Christina. If she ever saw the nanny again a murder would be committed.

Vittorio was sitting on the edge of the sofa, a brandy in one hand, his other occupied with drying his soaking-wet hair with a towel. The oil lamp was lit, throwing warm shadows across the room. Lili was aware of the still persistent beat of rain outside.

'I had to come,' he grated without looking at her. 'There are things that have to be said.'

'Yes, you could say that,' Lili responded brittly. 'And blame apportioned. What has happened is intolerable and the sooner you sort it out, the better.'

She had managed to stay reasonably calm after putting Carlo to bed. There had been no one to vent her fury on anyway. But now there was. Vittorio was here, the father of that adorable child upstairs, and she wasn't going to hold back even though none of this was her business.

He looked at her then, eyes blazing angrily, the pulse at his jawline throbbing so wildly that it inflamed Lili's anger even more. 'And don't look at me as if this has everything to do with me, Vittorio. The fault lies on your doorstep and no one else's.'

He looked confused for a second and then retorted sharply, 'And don't try to shift the blame exclusively to me. I'm not damned well perfect and nor are you. What happened was inevitable; neither of us could have stopped it.'

He thrust the towel impatiently aside, lifted the brandy to his lips, and something inside Lili snapped. How could he try and twist out of this and how could he possibly see any justification in trying to swing some of the blame on to her? She wasn't the boy's mother or his nanny!

Her hand came down and sliced at the glass, knocking it to the ground, where it shattered into a thousand fragments. 'What on earth has got into you? Haven't you a gram of feeling in that cold heart of yours?' she seethed furiously.

His anger flared as swiftly as a bush fire in a mistral and suddenly he was on his feet and wrenching at her, to pull her into his arms.

'And you, where are your feelings, where is your heart?' he grated painfully. 'I came here tonight to be with you because the last few days without you have been hell, and I'm greeted by stiff accusations instead of warm understanding.'

Lili went slack in his arms, suddenly realising what was happening. They were arguing at cross purposes. He didn't know. Vittorio Rossi didn't know that his son wasn't at home but upstairs sleeping.

'Vittorio!' she exclaimed. 'Vittorio, listen to me——'

'I've listened enough. There is only one language to get through to you.' His lips were hard on hers and Lili didn't know whether to laugh or cry. He had come to her because he didn't want it to end, because he wanted to be with her, and she should be elated, but now . . . now wasn't the time.

She tore her mouth from his. 'Please, Vittorio,' her voice came in a harsh pleading whisper, and she had to swallow hard to ease her throat. 'You haven't been home, have you? Carlo——'

She didn't finish for Vittorio's whole body stiffened alarmingly.

'Carlo?' he bellowed and in that moment Lili knew he loved his son more than life itself.

'He's here,' she blurted quickly, gripping his arms to steady him. 'He's upstairs in my father's bedroom, sleeping. He's perfectly safe. He was alone in the house, the storm came and he was afraid——'

Again she didn't finish, for there was a roar like an animal in pain and then Vittorio was gone, across the room in a stride and heading upstairs in bounds.

Lili kneaded her hot brow and slowly went to the kitchen to make coffee. The brandy bottle was on the side where Vittorio had left it after helping himself, and she slurped a shot into two cups while water boiled for the coffee.

She ached to think she had doubted Vittorio Rossi's love for his son, only briefly, but it brought it painfully home to her how little she knew about him. She shouldn't have doubted; she should have known he couldn't have been home to discover the absence of his son. He had come straight to her after his business trip and she should feel elated by that, but the feeling couldn't come because there was a sad little boy upstairs who needed his father more than she did.

'What happened?'

Lili turned and was shocked to see the whiteness of his face, the sudden gauntness sagging his face and ageing him beyond his years. His years—she didn't even know how old he was. Calmly Lili explained what had happened as she stirred the coffee in the jug and then poured it through a filter over the brandy. She felt no twist of conscience as she condemned Christina. A child's life had been threatened this night because of her.

'I'm just glad I was here,' she finished. She looked deeply into Vittorio's eyes. 'I'm glad he trusted me enough to come to me.'

Vittorio held her eyes and Lili tried to understand, but there was too much pent-up anger in them to see beyond the glittering jet.

'How could this have happened?' he seethed brutally. His fists balled threateningly and then he broke into fiery Italian and rattled on, occasionally yelling Christina's name, till the colour came back to his face.

'Wow, I'm glad I wasn't on the receiving-end of *that*,' Lili sighed, feigning relief when he was finished.

'It's not amusing,' he gravelled. Not all his anger was abated by his outburst.

'No, it's not,' she mumbled. 'Sorry; I didn't mean to be facetious.' She smiled suddenly and warmly, hoping to melt that last shard of anger from him.

'It's over now. Carlo is safe and we should be grateful for that. Do you feel better now?' She handed him his coffee.

He nodded and his hand was shaking as he took the cup from her. Lili took her coffee and the brandy bottle to the sofa and Vittorio followed her, sitting on the edge, on alert as if Carlo would wake at any moment and cry out for him.

'He could have died,' he murmured desperately.

'Don't torture yourself with that thought,' Lili told him reassuringly. 'He could only have been out in the rain fifteen minutes and it's pretty warm out there.'

'You treated the wound on his head?'

'It's only a graze. He stumbled in the mud.'

He fell into silence, staring down at his coffee, his eyes moist with concern, his thoughts somewhere inaccessible to Lili. 'She told me he wasn't mine, you know,' he breathed at last.

Stunned, Lili watched in silence as he poured more brandy into his coffee. He was going to get drunk and Lili didn't try to stop him. He'd had a shock but Carlo was safe; now he wanted to talk and Lili wanted to listen because she loved him so much and badly wanted to help.

'Christina told you——'

He shook his head. 'No, my wife.'

Lili's heart twisted painfully. 'Your . . . your wife told you Carlo wasn't your child?' Her voice was barely above a whisper.

He smiled wryly. 'Have you ever seen a son more like his father?'

Lili laughed softly in agreement. 'So why did she say something that wasn't true?'

'That was her scheme of things. The marriage was going badly and she wanted a divorce. I wouldn't allow it. I made a marriage for better or worse. I told you I don't believe in divorce.' He laughed softly and turned his head to look into her misty hazel eyes. 'I know what you are thinking because you are your father's daughter. Hugo thought me a fool but he respected my views. When she died he was a great help to me in dealing with it.'

'Did you love her very much?' Lili asked softly, secretly praying he hadn't. It was silly but she felt such envy for a woman who had shared part of Vittorio Rossi's life and borne him such a beautiful son.

'I thought I did. I was young, enraptured by her wit and culture, but I was never enough for her. I had money enough for her, but she didn't like the life here in the Tuscan hills. She wanted Milan— the fashion, the style, the glitz. Love was never enough for her. She eventually killed any feelings I had for her with her discontent.'

Lili began to see why he had felt such deep envy for her father and Emilia—true love on his very doorstep while his own relationship floundered helplessly.

'How did she die?' Lili asked bravely and then smiled impishly. 'Did you murder her in a fit of passion when she told you Carlo wasn't yours?'

Vittorio rolled his coffee-cup in the palms of his hands and smiled as he stared down at the rim. 'You're getting to know me very well.'

Lili looked mystified.

He looked up and laughed softly at her expression. 'I meant that you know me well enough to know that the brandy has mellowed me and I won't be offended by such an accusation.'

She smiled with him. 'And you know me well enough to know that I wasn't serious. I don't think for a minute that you bumped off your wife. But in your shoes I think I would have done the dastardly deed and then made a break for it.' What a blow to a man's ego to be told the child he loved wasn't his.

'But I was responsible for her death in a way...' he went on. Lili fidgeted uncomfortably. Guilt was a terrible problem to deal with, unresolvable to some. 'I bought her a mare for our wedding anniversary. She loved it and I thought we were making a breakthrough in our marriage, but she insisted on riding alone. It wasn't long before she grew bored with it. One night after a particularly painful row she told me she met her lover out riding. They made love in the hills, she said.' Vittorio smiled suddenly when Lili thought he ought to look grave. 'I never knew for sure if it was true or not but Hugo said it wasn't very likely as no man would dare make love to the wife of Vittorio Rossi, certainly not in the open where discovery by a peasant was likely, and, worse, an invasion of ants to dampen the ardour a constant threat.'

Lili laughed lightly. 'Yes, I can imagine my father saying that. Go on.'

'She kept up the taunting till I was half crazed with suppressed anger. Then she told me Carlo wasn't my son but her lover's child. I was incensed, but to show such rage would have delighted her.

She went on and on and then she screamed that she was going to meet him that very night.' Vittorio bowed his head and gazed at the floor. 'I should have stopped her,' he grazed softly. 'She went and never came back. We found her next morning, high in the hills, the mare grazing near by.'

'The . . . the horse threw her?' Lili anticipated in an impassioned whisper.

'The terrain was rough, the mare skittish; it could have stumbled and thrown her. In her troubled mind she could have over-exerted the animal. No one knows.' His voice lowered. 'Her neck was broken. She didn't suffer; it was instantaneous.'

Lili didn't know what to say. Like Vittorio she clasped her coffee-cup in her hands and stared down at it. She felt his pain and understood his guilt. It hadn't been his fault but the circumstances leading up to her death must have filled him with regret forevermore.

Vittorio was the first to speak after a long pause. 'Your father was a great support to me at the time. I blamed myself, of course, but he talked me through it for hours, weeks, months. Eventually he lessened and eased my guilt. He was the wisest man I had ever met.' He smiled again and shook his head. 'He used to talk about you a lot. We all longed to meet you.'

'And yet he never contacted me in my adolescence,' Lili murmured. She looked at Vittorio. 'Was there a reason for that?' she asked softly. 'Did Emilia stop him doing that?'

Vittorio shook his dark head. 'Emilia would never have done that. She tried to persuade him to invite you here but although he might have been wise in many respects he was foolish in that way. He said there was plenty of time, that one day...' Vittorio let out a ragged sigh. 'Time ran out. His heart attack was totally unexpected.'

'How...how did it happen?' Lili asked. 'I never knew, you see. There was no one to tell me, just my mother who didn't know very much and by then didn't care very much anyway. I just knew that he'd had a heart attack, not where or why or how.'

He looked at her, dark eyes cloudy with fatigue and concern. He ran his tongue across his lips before telling her, 'He died here, in this room; it was very quick.'

Lili put her cup down on the floor and clutched her arms about her for comfort, staring at the candles burning low in the grate. She forced a smile through pale lips and mumbled to herself, 'I should have known that.' She remembered when Stefano Bellini had been here and she'd thought someone had blown on her neck. She'd never believed in ghosts before, but who knew?

'When I first came here you said my father had left me this place to teach me the values of life.' She turned to face him. 'Did he really? Or was that just your interpretation of events?'

Vittorio leaned back into the sofa and closed his eyes. 'Your father loved you but he didn't want to complicate your life by making demands on you, trying to pull you in a different direction, maybe unwittingly drawing you away from your mother. He knew how she felt about Emilia and he thought it best to leave things as they were till you were older.'

Vittorio opened his eyes and lifted a hand to stroke the back of her neck. 'There is no doubt in my mind that if he hadn't died suddenly he would have made contact with you, but he was also worried that you wouldn't understand his chosen life and what motivated him to shut himself away from the world here in the Tuscan hills.'

'So...so he left me the villa to show me,' Lili supposed softly.

The pressure on the back of her neck increased. 'I'm sure it was his very intention.'

But it was all so very vague, Lili mused to herself. If Vittorio Rossi hadn't been here she would never have known of the great love between Hugo and Emilia. And of course if Emilia had lived the villa wouldn't have been left to her anyway. Hugo *couldn't* have known that Emilia would die so soon after him, unless of course they were so close to each other and their love so powerfully paralleled that a life and death apart was unthinkable. And then to fully appreciate those values of life you needed to be here and be in love, and her father could never, never have envisaged that his daughter would fall in love with his great friend Vittorio Rossi and know and understand what he had experienced in this love-nest.

Vittorio's hand slackened from the rhythmic caress on her neck and Lili turned, expecting him to have fallen asleep. He was still awake—just— and smiling at her.

'And you have learned those values and you're not still thinking of selling, are you?' he said quietly.

'You told me I couldn't.' She wondered if he had lied about the land to keep her here. It was quite an exciting thought.

'I did, didn't I?' he uttered non-committally.

'Is that why you came straight here from your business trip—to make sure I wasn't still considering it?' There was just a slight inflexion of hurt in her tone.

His hand slid down her arm to her wrist and he lifted her hand to place it on his heart. 'I came here because of this, because I couldn't stay away a second longer.' He pulled her into his arms and his mouth was no denial of what he'd just said. The kiss was warm and sensual and as demanding as his heart.

Lili was lost in it till good sense outweighed desire. She wanted him so very much, body and soul, but how far was he committed to her? Somehow that was very important, and so were so many other things, like the small boy sleeping upstairs.

'Vittorio,' she murmured, parting her lips reluctantly from his, yet spurred by a small flame of anger that he could think of such a thing at such a time. 'Carlo is upstairs——'

He lowered his mouth to her throat and told her softly, 'The boy never wakes——'

'How would you know?'

It was out before she could reign it in, a silly, silly outburst born out of a fear that all he wanted was her body and not her heart and soul.

He stiffened against her and in embarrassment Lili pulled away and got to her feet. 'I'm sorry.' She raked her hair from her face. 'I'm really sorry for that. It just slipped out. I'm tired and I was worried about Carlo and . . . and, well, I think we should be discussing him and not——'

'And not making love?'

Her eyes stung as she stared down at him. This wasn't going to sound very 'nineties' but out it was going to come all the same. 'And that is what you came for, wasn't it?' she sighed hurtfully.

She must be going mad. Had she really said that? she wondered as his eyes glazed furiously, acknowledging that she had. Why was she doing this, ruining it all, saying things she didn't mean?

Vittorio stood up to face her, his features grey in the dim light from the oil lamp as he fought back that fury. 'And that was such a very female accusation that I refuse to comment on it for its sheer absurdity value. You are right in one respect, though—Carlo is my first concern. I'll take him home now.'

Lili bit her lip with remorse and quickly touched his arm, letting her fingers linger. Her eyes were wide and appealing, so deeply regretting her silly, silly outburst. Her mouth softened into a small smile. 'Can an absurd female apologise? I'm sorry, Vittorio. I'm tired and so are you and . . . and you can't disturb your son at this hour. . .' Her voice frayed and then she drew courage and whispered, 'Leave him to rest and stay yourself.' She shook her head slightly. 'I don't . . . I don't mean that as . . . as an invitation to make love——'

'No, of course not,' he interrupted brutally, that searing Italian blood of his so quickly to the boil again. But as swiftly as it rose it fell, leaving him looking more exhausted than ever. 'I came here to talk, Lili,' he added.

'I know,' she uttered sympathetically, 'and I want to talk too, but we're both exhausted and in the morning Carlo will want his *papà* in a good humour, not like this—mad as a bear with a sore head.'

She hoped he'd understand. He stood before her, tall, strong, very much the arrogant dark stranger who had stepped out of the shadows the day she had arrived. She should have known then that he would have a devastating effect on her life. He was exciting and very endearingly pigheaded and so very easily provoked into a rage, but he adored his son, and a man like that...

'Stay,' she pleaded softly. 'Tomorrow we can talk. Sleep in my room; you'll be closer to Carlo if he awakes. It will be better if Carlo finds you alone in my bed and not both of us.'

He gazed down at her, the fury abated. His hands took her shoulders. 'I haven't finished with you yet, Lili Mayer. I'm amazed at your feeble attempts at dominance, amazed at your feeble outspokenness, but I thank you for your good sense,' he teased. His mouth touched hers, so lightly, so wearily that she smiled on the kiss.

After washing up the coffee-cups, she took a dustpan and brush and swept up the glass she had shattered from his hand. The candles in the grate were burnt down to waxy stumps and she blew them out before slumping back into the sofa. She'd heard him moving about her room and finally settling for the night, and now all was silent. The rain had ceased and the air was fresher but she knew she wouldn't sleep. She lay in the stillness and thought of ways to make it right with Vittorio. But to what purpose? Love? Marriage? What was Vittorio looking for? What was she looking for? All she knew for certain was that she loved him. He wanted her, she knew that, but maybe not for life. The man was chasing an idyll, searching for what Hugo and Emilia had had—perfection. Their love had been unique, Lili had supposed, but now she knew differently. A love like that wasn't. It was available to those who let it into their hearts. Lili was already committed, body and soul. If only the subject of her adoration could commit his heart too.

Later, Lili stood at the foot of her father's bed and gazed down at Carlo still sleeping so peacefully. She held a new candle in her hand and it cast a soft light on the child's face. He was beautiful, Vittorio's son.

'What shall I do?' she murmured into the stillness. She waited for the soft breath on the back of her neck but nothing happened. 'So much for ghosts,' she mumbled ruefully, and crept out of the room.

She stopped outside her own room. The door was ajar and as she held the candle aloft she was able to see Vittorio sleeping under the thin cotton sheet. In that moment she imagined what her father's purpose was in leaving her this villa and her imagination soared to such a fantasy that she convinced herself it was true. Her father and Vittorio had been great friends, had probably loved each other like a father and son. Hugo would have suffered with Vittorio every inch of the way of his desperate marriage and he would have wanted him to find happiness, maybe a part of the happiness he shared with Emilia. Maybe he thought Vittorio would find that happiness with his very own daughter!

The fantasy engulfed Lili, swamped her, drowned her till she gasped with the certainty of it all. This was meant to be. Lili and Vittorio.

She knew then what she had to do. She had to love this man, because if you didn't give you didn't receive. She blew out the candle and waited for her eyes to accustom to the darkness. Silently she closed the door after her and crossed the room to stand by the bed. Her fingers were trembling as she fumbled with her robe, and as she let it drop to the floor she bit her lip at the desire that was already vaporising on her heated flesh. She touched her warm breasts with the tips of her fingers, already anticipating the effect of his caresses. Her skin was on fire, her pulses racing, and the ache deep within her could only be satisfied by this man she loved.

Lili slid into bed beside him, her whole body going into a spasm of desperate need as their heated flesh made contact. He let out a small moan as if disturbed by a fretful nightmare but he didn't awaken. Lili ran her tremulous hands over his chest, down to his stomach and across his hips. She leaned up and gazed down at him, feeling the contours of his face with the tips of her fingers. She lowered her head to feather kisses across his taut jawline, to release that anger-pulse of his, to awaken him with her need.

At last he turned to her, letting out a long breath of surprise and desire and then she had to do no more as he enfolded her in his arms, his kisses so rawly passionate that she thrilled at the speed of his arousal.

'*Amore*,' he breathed heavily against her throat. 'This time...'

His lovemaking was pure adoration, a form of heavenly worship she had never thought possible between a man and a woman. His smooth, skilled caresses and teasing tongue elevated her to a sphere beyond the heavens. Lili was light-headed, drunk with desire, not on this worldly plane at all. He drew erotically on her breasts till she had to seal the cry of joy in her throat in case she woke the world.

She wanted him inside her, she wanted the completeness to be absolute, she wanted to let go and cry and sob and tear at him. She tried to touch him but he moaned softly against her and moved out of reach.

'Vittorio,' she husked desperately and then she understood, but understanding didn't help the desperate need for his penetration. And then a new sensation rippled deep within her, a new feeling that she had never experienced before in her life—eroticism. His tongue teased and slicked down from her swollen breasts, down across her stomach, delicately across her sensitive scar. She gasped as gently he parted her thighs and ran his hot lips across the soft, sensitive triangle of silky hair that protected her inner sweetness.

Lili's back arched and her small white teeth crunched hard on her lower lip to stop the cry in her swollen throat. Hot liquid fire enveloped every pulse of her being. There was no life, no future, nothing beyond the glory of his mouth adoring her so intimately. Her legs were boneless, her whole body traumatised with the sheer exquisiteness of these tiny erotic thrusts she was moving her hips against.

'Oh, God,' she moaned, her head thrashing from side to side as his tongue penetrated deeper and she could hold back no longer. 'Please, Vittorio, please,' she implored.

She clawed at his shoulders and he responded instantly, his head coming up and then crushing down on her pulsing throat. At that instant he penetrated her deeply, so completely that she came immediately, a hot, hot rush of molten adoration for this man who ground into her so passionately. In that desperate, totally fulfilling rush of sensation his mouth moved to hers and she parted her lips and tasted her own passionate scent on his. It mingled with the secret taste of him and bonded her life with his forevermore.

It was then that Vittorio started to murmur in Italian, words she didn't understand but which nevertheless excited her senses. He moved more urgently into her and as she clung to him in his final thrusts she heard two words she did understand. '*Ti amo*,' was torn from his throat and then his climax hit them both and Lili's mouth ground against his to smother the roar of ecstasy that came from deep in his chest. They shuddered together, clung together and were one in that moment of completeness.

Lili awoke to strange sounds: the clatter of china, muted laughter, a swoosh of water. The only sound that was familiar was the cicadas buzzing like mini chain-saws in the fig tree outside.

Carlo, Vittorio, Vittorio, Carlo, here together in her father's home. Lili stretched lazily. It seemed they had more right to it than she. She frowned and bunched the pillow under her head. Why did she feel so desperately alone? She shouldn't after last night; she should feel part of them. Both had come to her in their hour of need; both had *needed* her.

She rose and went to the bathroom and heard them laughing below. They didn't sound as if they needed her now. She sighed and brushed her shoulder-length tawny hair till her scalp hurt. It was question-and-answer time, the morning after the night before when doubt swept away euphoria. First the pleasure, then the pain. Lili shook herself determinedly. She mustn't think like this, but insecurity was another difficult-to-deal-with emotion. Why couldn't she accept that Vittorio loved her? After last night she should be walking on air.

She drew in a determined breath. What she was going to do was breeze downstairs and give the two men in her life a big hug and everything but everything would be all right.

She did nothing of the sort when she stepped into the long room and saw them both in the kitchen. Bright sunshine glanced off the tops of the two Rossi heads. Carlo was sitting cross-legged on the work surface swamped in one of Lili's baggy T-shirts and nothing else. Vittorio was making coffee and spreading bread thickly with honey. They spoke together in Italian, sharing a joke, not seeing her across the room.

Lili needed that hug now. She needed someone to make her feel wanted, for that old feeling of not being a part of anyone's life was creeping up on her again.

Vittorio looked up suddenly and beamed. 'Lili, we have a big problem. Carlo has no clean clothes and he absolutely refuses to get off this kitchen-top without any pants...' Carlo cried out in embarrassment and punched at his father. Vittorio feigned hurt and they laughed together.

'I'm sorry,' Lili said brightly, forcing herself jauntily across the room. 'I should have been up all night scrubbing clothes, polishing floors——'

'Ah, poor Cinderella,' Vittorio teased. 'What shall we do to make her happy, Buttons?' he directed at his son.

Carlo thought for only a second. 'The prince must marry her!' he shouted.

'Haven't you forgotten something?' Vittorio asked him, frowning deeply, but his eyes twinkling.

Carlo shrieked and pointed at Lili's bare feet. 'She hasn't any shoes. She must have glass slippers.' He was so involved in the play-acting that his face grew solemn. 'But we haven't any glass slippers——!' he cried mournfully.

'Nor a Prince Charming!' Lili cut in ruefully.

Vittorio lifted an empty jar from the work surface. 'Look, we have a glass slipper.'

'And Papà is the prince!' Carlo cried at the top of his voice, flinging one arm around his father's neck and the other round Lili's.

They were all laughing by the time he let them go but only one heart was tearing. If only fairy-tales came true.

'I can't go home without any pants, Lili,' Carlo wailed as he let them go. 'I'll have to stay here *all day* till you wash and dry and iron my dirty clothes.'

Lili planted a kiss on the boy's forehead. 'Oh, you are your father's son,' she crooned, stinging Vittorio with a waspish glare. 'OK, I won't scream, "Sexist!" I'll pound away all day on my washing slab and send you home decent.'

Carlo whooped and hugged her and Lili held Vittorio's eyes over the boy's shoulder. She saw warmth and love and her heart spun, and she nearly hugged Carlo to death, then she swung him down to the floor, pulling the T-shirt nearly down to his ankles. 'There—modesty prevails; now do something for me. Take a carton of milk from the fridge for the cats and disappear for four days; I want to talk to your father.'

'Four days!' the boy cried as he did as he was told. 'I can't live for four days without my pants!'

Vittorio and Lili laughed as he hurried out of the door and then there was no more laughter as Vittorio swept her into his arms. The kiss was wonderful and allayed all her fears, but not quite all the doubts. For until Vittorio repeated what he had said in his moment of joy in the night she wouldn't know for certain if she had imagined it or not.

'Were you up before Carlo woke?' was the first question she asked when their lips parted at last.

'There's a leading question.'

'Vittorio!' Lili howled.

'Serves you right for asking such a *romantic* question,' he grazed sarcastically at her throat.

'How could I be romantic when I'm confronted with a pile of washing first thing in the morning?' she laughed.

'That's *la dolce vita*, I'm afraid,' he teased.

She playfully pinched his shoulders. If only he would repeat what he had said in the night. *Ti amo*—I love you. Had she misheard, misinterpreted, or simply missed the point that things were said in the heat of passion and not meant to be taken as gospel in the cool of reality?

Vittorio held her by the shoulders and suddenly his dark eyes were serious. 'Lili, I have to go up to my home, to see Christina——'

'If she's there,' Lili interjected, not meaning it to sound peevish, but still she couldn't believe what that woman had done.

'If she isn't I must find her anyway. I can't understand what could have happened...'

Lili thought she did. Poor Christina, loving Vittorio and him not noticing, driven to the depths of drink by a love that wasn't returned. Yes, Lili understood and sympathised.

'I have to deal with this and...and there is no one to care for——'

'Carlo,' Lili finished for him. She grinned. 'He's already manipulated himself into staying for the day.'

Vittorio smiled. 'He is smarter than his father. He is very fond of you, Lili, and that is very good. It makes it all so much easier.' His mouth came down to hers and Lili had no chance to interpret what exactly he meant by that. She forgot it as his mouth offered her so much. She clung to him, smoothing her hands in his hair, pressing her warm body against the urgency of his.

'I wish I could stay,' he murmured deeply at last, drawing back from her and smoothing a strand of her hair from her cheek, 'but you understand that I must go.'

Lili nodded regretfully. 'Yes, you must go. Carlo is perfectly safe with me.'

He kissed her lightly and then he was gone, and Lili was left feeling oddly empty and dissatisfied because he hadn't said when he would return. But she was wrong to feel that way when he had already given so much. He did care, deeply, and to believe he didn't was so...so very female. Insecurity again, Lili thought as she went to find Carlo, born out of not having a father to guide her way; but knowing that sometimes didn't help—like now when she needed reassurance so much and there was no one on hand to offer it.

'The kittens must have come in the night,' Carlo whispered reverentially as Lili squatted down with him next to the cardboard box. She'd found him where she guessed she would and without knowing it the boy would be her reassurance.

'Hear how the mother purrs,' Lili whispered as she gazed down at the four tiny lumps of damp fur that suckled their mother.

'Because she is happy,' Carlo told her wisely. 'Papà says my *mamma* was very happy when she had me. She wanted a boy because she loved Papà so.'

A sharp pain caught Lili between the shoulder-blades. It hurt badly, stinging her eyes so that they misted, and she could hardly see the kittens suckling so greedily.

'And Papà loved her too,' Carlo went on, 'and he said that even if someone is dead the loving doesn't stop.'

Slowly, painfully Lili stood up. The kittens were a blur, Carlo was a blur. The sun beat on the top of her head and it was the only physical sensation she could register.

At last she murmured, 'I'd better go and rinse your clothes.' She went inside the villa where it was cool and dim and the desolation that swamped her was complete. Lili Mayer was no part of their lives. There was no place in Vittorio's heart for another love; he still lived with the original one and he always would.

CHAPTER EIGHT

'WHAT'S the Rossi boy doing here?' Stefano Bellini asked as he slammed shut his car door.

Both Carlo and Lili had heard a car pull up on the gravel late in the afternoon. Carlo had shot round the side of the villa to see if it was his father but Lili had held back in the shadows of an olive tree. She was in no hurry to come face to face with Vittorio again. It was all different now.

Disappointed, Carlo had scurried back to the outer courtyard feeling it his earthbound duty to watch over the kittens all day. Lili stepped out of the shadows to greet the solicitor.

'Visiting,' she told him, though wondering why she needed to answer to him. 'Vittorio has some business to attend to.'

'Yes, with the beautiful Christina; I've just seen them driving down the mountain road.' Stefano laughed cynically. 'And Lili is left holding the baby.'

Lili refused to respond to that implication. 'Yes, he has business with Christina.'

'And we know just what sort, don't we? And we too have business,' he said in such a suggestive tone that it churned Lili's stomach. 'I think we ought to discuss it over a cooling glass of wine, don't you?'

'Why not?' Lili smiled. It would give her great pleasure to tell him what he didn't want to hear. She almost felt sorry for him as he followed her through the villa to the shady patio courtyard. He was very likely going to take the full brunt of her disillusionment over Vittorio.

She poured two glasses of wine at the rustic table and sat down to face him.

'You have looked over the contracts?'

'No,' Lili told him. 'I see no point as I'm not going to sell.'

Stefano swallowed hard before saying anything then he said tightly, 'If you want more money——'

'I don't want *any* money, Stefano. I'm not going to sell and, besides, I think you've overlooked something. The land under this villa doesn't go with the property. It still belongs to Vittorio Rossi. I'm not free to sell to you if I wanted to, which I don't!'

Stefano laughed thinly. 'The land is all I'm interested in, Lili. It's a huge plot. I could get quite a few units up here. Tourists are spreading into the Tuscan hills and snapping up properties. You don't think I would have made such an incredible offer for this old heap of stones.' His narrowed eyes flicked disdainfully towards the villa and Lili personally felt the stab of humiliation and rejection for the old house. 'Who told you the land wasn't a part of the property, Vittorio himself? The man takes us both for fools.'

'Are you saying he's a liar?' Lili breathed hesitantly. Incredible as it was, she didn't know who to believe any more.

'I don't need to say it. I know it. I have the deeds. The Villa Libra and the land it occupies was a gift from Vittorio Rossi to Hugo Mayer. Your father left you this property and it is yours, to do with as you will and, Lili, you would be a fool not to take my offer. No one else would make you such a generous one.' He frowned suddenly. 'Unless, of course, Vittorio has.'

'No,' Lili murmured. 'He hasn't made me an offer.' Not the one she so yearned for.

Stefano raised a sun-bleached brow. 'Maybe he is coming to his senses at last . . .' And then a smile of dawning broke across his face. Lili watched him warily. 'Or maybe he has bewitched you . . .' Suddenly he slapped the table-top. 'Ah, yes, I see it now. The boy here . . .'

Just then the boy appeared. 'Lili, the mother cat is crying. I think she's hungry.'

'Take some milk from the fridge, Carlo,' Lili told him.

Carlo hovered, reluctant to leave. 'Lili, Papà is late.' His eyes were bright with anticipation. 'Does that mean we can stay another night?'

From out of the mouths of babes . . . Lili wanted to fold into the ground. She didn't look at Stefano; she didn't have to to know what he was thinking. 'Hurry with the milk, Carlo. The mother will need a lot of nourishment while she is feeding.'

Carlo scampered off, his concern for the new mother outweighing his need to know if he was allowed another night at the Villa Libra.

'I see,' Stefano crowed, helping himself to more wine.

'Yes, you see,' Lili flaunted deliberately. She wasn't going to deny it; there was no point. 'Carlo was here last night, and his father—both of them, all night.'

Stefano laughed bitterly. 'And that has influenced your decision not to sell?' He shook his head in disbelief. 'Lili, I thought more of you——'

'He's a very attractive man and when in Rome and all that, why not?' Her chin came up defiantly. 'But it has nothing to do with my not wanting to sell to you. This was my father's home——'

'This has nothing to do with your father, Lili. That Rossi bastard has seduced you and you think you are in with a chance. It's not possible, *cara*. Has he told you about his wife?'

'As it happens, yes,' Lili answered stiffly.

'And yet still he adored her and still does. All of Tuscany knew what she was like but he stood by her; the idiot couldn't see what was staring him in the face——'

Lili stood up, trembling from head to toe. 'I really don't care to hear any more of your petty gossip. You came here for my decision and I've given it to you. I'm not selling. Not now, not ever. This was my father's home and because of him——'

'You're beginning to sound like Rossi,' he interrupted angrily, 'full of pretentious sentimentality.' Stefano Bellini stood up. 'The man is sick, the whole family was sick——'

'It's time you went, Stefano,' Lili ordered levelly, incredibly controlled in spite of the rage that shook her insides.

Stefano leered across at her. 'I bet you didn't say that to Rossi last night. Well, if you're handing out favours, consider me next in line.' He reached across the table to her and Lili was so taken by surprise that she had no time to move out of the way. Bellini caught her wrist and pulled her against him. Lili caught her thigh on the edge of the table and cried out. Her cry was suffocated by his wet mouth on hers. She struggled furiously, which did nothing to deter the force of him. His grasp on her was painful and terrifying. His hand went to tear at the neck of her shirt, his mouth grazing furiously on hers, drawing blood inside her mouth.

Lili sobbed out loud and clenched her fist to throw a punch at him. He caught her arm and twisted it painfully behind her while his other hand brazenly cupped her breast. His mouth scorched over hers once more and Lili retched with the sweetness of it, and as her mouth opened to scream in terror she was cut short by the frantic peal of a bell.

The deafening sound stopped life instantly. Stefano Bellini froze, stricken by the dense peal that reverberated round the small courtyard. Lili clutched her ears and squeezed her eyes tightly shut and prayed for the world to stop spinning.

When eventually she let her hands drop and opened her eyes, Bellini had gone. There was only a small sound from the outer courtyard, a small, inhuman cry, and then the revving of a car engine and hot tyres grazing fearfully on gravel.

Lili was stunned for a few seconds, not understanding, not having the strength to move, and then realisation hit her and she remembered last night and a small boy protesting that Nonna had rung the bell...

Carlo was slumped beneath the bell, crumpled in a heap and sobbing quietly. Lili crouched down and feverishly gathered him into her arms, and he clung to her, terrified and suddenly so very small and vulnerable.

'It's all right, Carlo, darling, it's all right,' she whispered raggedly. Oh, God, what had the boy heard and seen?

'I...I...wanted him to stop. He...he was...hurting you...'

She smoothed her trembling fingers down the side of his face. 'It's all right, Carlo. I'm all right. You...you did the right thing.' But Vittorio wouldn't come. She didn't know where he was; according to Bellini he was on the mountain road with Christina. At this moment she couldn't even begin to wonder why.

'I...I didn't want to ring...the bell...I *hate* the bell. Nonna rang the bell when...Nonno died. I...hate the bell.'

Oh, no, not that! Lili clung to him, her own tears rushing now. He must have been about five...

Lili was the first to hear the sound of the car, its engine racing, coming from the direction of the village. She tensed against the small boy, knowing it was Vittorio but not knowing how she was going to explain what had happened.

'Papà!' Carlo cried and tore himself from Lili's arms and ran to the front of the villa. Slowly Lili stood up. Her mouth hurt and she brushed her fingers gingerly across her lips and stared down at the smear of blood. She couldn't face Vittorio, not yet, but there was nowhere to run to. She wiped the blood down the sides of her shorts, rubbed ferociously at her thigh where she had caught it on the table and with her head held high she walked into the house, across the long room to the foot of the stairs.

Vittorio's roar stopped her dead before she could get her foot on the bottom step.

'Lili, what's happened?'

She turned slowly. Carlo had by now given him most of the sordid story, she supposed. Perhaps later she would tell her side, but not now. She felt sick to the pit of her stomach and just wanted to be on her own.

She licked her sore lips and spoke softly. 'Nothing happened, thanks to your son; he's a hero. Look after him, Vittorio; he needs you at the moment, far more than I do.' She walked slowly up the stairs and Vittorio didn't stop her.

Lili locked herself in the bathroom and her hands shook so much that she could hardly get her clothes off. Her chest was sore with trying to hold back the sobs, her throat raging with fever. She could still taste Bellini's mouth, that acrid sweetness. She flew to the sink and filled her mouth with water and spat and spat till she could spit no more. What would have happened if Carlo hadn't rung the bell? And all her own fault. By admitting that she'd spent the night with Vittorio she'd asked for it. No! To hell with it; she hadn't asked for it and she damn well wasn't going to carry the blame and the guilt.

'Lili, open the door.' Vittorio's voice was surprisingly calm. 'Please open it, Lili. Carlo told me what happened——'

'Where is Carlo?' she croaked. She couldn't bear it if the boy was with him, to witness more of her humiliation.

'In the car with Gina, a girl who comes up to help at the villa sometimes. I'd been to collect her and we were on our way up when I heard the bell.'

Poor little soul, Lili thought hotly, pushed from pillar to post by a succession of relatives and helpers.

'Lili, listen to me. I'm taking Carlo home——'

Lili clamped her hand to her mouth to suppress a sob. Yes, he must, but her own need cried out too. She wanted him to stay and hold her and tell her it was all going to be all right.

Lili steadied herself at the sink and breathed deeply. 'Yes, you must take him...' Her voice broke and the strength went from her.

Suddenly the door burst at the flimsy lock and Vittorio Rossi filled the room. He pulled her naked form feverishly into his arms, burying his mouth in her tousled hair. He was shaking and Lili clung to him, sobbing quietly. 'Please, Vittorio, I'm...I'm OK...I'm all right and...and Carlo needs you.'

His mouth grazed a soft kiss over her brow. 'I know, and I'm torn between the two of you——'

'Don't be,' she urged, bringing her hands up to rest against his chest. Oh, God, but she needed him, more than he would ever know. Why wasn't there ever anyone there for her? She bit her lips fiercely, her injured lip, and it started the blood seeping again. 'You must go to Carlo, Vittorio. He's had a shock and he needs calming down. I'm fine, honestly. I'm going to take a shower.'

He closed his eyes for a second as if struggling to make a decision and then he opened them again and nodded. 'Yes, do that,' he agreed tenderly. 'I'll be back, Lili.' He kissed her forehead and she

wanted to cling to him, but she held back, so fiercely
that the effort made her head swim. And then he
was gone and she was so sick at the sink that she
didn't hear the car pull out of the driveway.

Lili showered, long and cool, and rubbed herself
till she ached with rawness. She dressed slowly in
a thin cotton sundress and brushed her hair out.
Her movements were thought about and done determinedly because to lose concentration would
mean collapse. She went downstairs and poured
herself a cold drink. She drank it outside at the
table, numbed against what had happened. Stefano
Bellini's attack on her was nothing. The love
Vittorio still had for his feckless wife was everything. Carlo had endorsed it, Bellini had confirmed it. Lili couldn't live with it.

'Lili!'
She heard his call but didn't respond. Her mouth
was sore, her thigh ached, her arm was stiff where
Bellini had wrenched at it. Otherwise she was very
well. Totally in command, resolute and knowing
exactly where she was going—home to England.

'Lili!' Vittorio opened the door of the study and
stopped dead. 'What are you doing?'

She turned to him from the desk. It was quite
remarkable what you could achieve when you tried,
she convinced herself. She didn't feel anything. He
was here and she didn't feel a thing. No rush of
emotions, no leap of the heart at the sight of him
so cool and dark and handsome. Yes, she could see
all that, acknowledge it and control it.

'I'm packing some of my father's papers to take back to England with me. The rest you can sort out, seeing as you were such buddies.'

She couldn't help the bitterness in her tone. You could go so far with control but then you were up against a barrier of pain. Even the envy of friendship between Vittorio and her father was something that would have to be fought and overpowered.

'What the hell has got into you?'

He came across the room and wrenched at her arm and Lili flinched with the pain. Regardless of it, she pulled away from him. 'Nothing has got into me, Vittorio. And don't sound so incredulous. You knew I would have to go home some time.'

'This is your home!'

Lili braved herself to look him straight in the face. She wavered for a split-second, just a micro-second as she met such deep pain in his dark eyes, but then the indecision was gone. She couldn't compete with his past even though he looked at her that way.

'This was my father's home, not mine, and don't waste your breath on the values-of-life soliloquy. I know where mine are and they aren't here.' She turned back to shuffling her father's papers into a neat pile.

There was a long silence as Lili worked and that surprised her. She had expected a storm of some sort. But of course he could only be angry if her leaving was cutting him up. He didn't care enough for her to be angry. She couldn't win.

'I do understand,' he said at last, softly, verging on patronisingly to Lili's ears. 'You had a bad experience with Bellini——'

Lili snorted and shoved the papers into a brown envelope. 'How could you possibly understand? Women don't go around indecently assaulting men——'

'Some do.' He smiled as he said that and Lili wished she had the capability of being able to smile with him. He was doing his best to lighten a very tricky situation.

'Vittorio,' she sighed, 'I don't even want to discuss it.'

'But you have to, and we have things to discuss too, but first we have to speak of Bellini. Tomorrow I deal with him, today you talk it out. It was a traumatic experience for you. Carlo told me what he knew. That Bellini was angry——'

'It was an unwelcome kiss, Vittorio Rossi; heaven knows I've suffered enough of them in my time. Just a wild kiss thrown out of frustration, very similar to the very one you first assaulted me with. No different. If Carlo hadn't rung the bell you wouldn't even have known about it.'

'Carlo said you were terrified——'

'Carlo is a child who doesn't know the difference between terrified and *excited*!' The retort came like a sabre-blade, intended to hurt, intended to end it all.

In a sudden fury Vittorio exploded into scathing Italian, swung round and hammered the back of the door with his fist.

'*Mamma mia*!' Lili mocked facetiously. 'You'd be a wow in a King's Road pizzeria—as a waiter,' she added hurtfully.

'I'm going to pour a drink,' he said through clenched teeth. 'I'm not leaving, because I haven't finished with you yet—no, not by a long way.'

Lili was filled with remorse as she heard him moving around the kitchen. She had insulted his Italian pride yet again. He'd done nothing to deserve such treatment. He wasn't to know she had fallen in love with him and every emotion in her body was on the surface of her skin just waiting to be scoured by innocent remarks made by innocent people. No, Bellini's scathing disclosure about Vittorio and the adoration of his discontented wife hadn't been spoken in innocence, it had been deliberately said to hurt. But not Carlo's revelation; that had truly been spoken in innocence and that had been the one that hurt most. Vittorio Rossi still loved his wife and death didn't stop the loving.

'How is Carlo?' she asked Vittorio.

He was stretched out on the sofa, reading a book propped against his thighs, one hand supporting the back of his head, the other supporting a glass of wine on his chest. It was too hot to be outside. Inside was cooler but dim because of the shutters at the windows keeping the last of the sun's rays at bay.

'How can you read in this light?' she added, flopping down on the other sofa, taking up a lotus position and gathering her skirt around her legs. How could he read at a time like this?

'I'm not reading, just staring at the words.' He tossed the book down on the floor but apart from that didn't move. 'I was thinking, about you and Carlo and myself and——'

'How is Carlo?' she repeated. She guessed his wife was about to be added to that list and she didn't want to hear it all again. She was more concerned for the boy.

'The child is very resilient; all children are. Tomorrow he will have forgotten all about it——'

'I doubt that,' Lili snapped cynically. 'The poor child still hasn't got over the last time the bell tolled.'

'What do you mean?' Vittorio grazed.

'My God,' Lili breathed desolately, glaring at him. 'You don't even know, do you?'

'Know what, for heaven's sake?' His eyes blazed angrily and the wine slopped on his shirt as he heaved himself up to a sitting position.

'You don't know anything!' Lili told him tightly. 'Absolutely nothing about the boy. You leave him in the care of some drunken distant cousin who is more concerned with bedding you and kicking cats than what she is paid to do.'

'Bedding me?' he cried in astonishment.

Lili stared at him and then lowered her head and wondered if she had been mistaken. 'I thought . . . I got the impression . . . that . . . that Christina wanted . . . wanted to be more than a nanny——'

'Don't be ridiculous,' he laughed.

Lili didn't think she was being ridiculous. But maybe Christina just had fire in her blood for any man—hence the reason for her leaving Carlo alone at night when Vittorio was away. Lili decided there was no point in bringing that up. Vittorio had dealt with it in his own way. Christina was gone and best forgotten.

'Back to the bell,' she went on tightly. 'Didn't you know Carlo was terrified of it?'

'No, I didn't.' He put his empty wine glass down on the floor, leaned his elbows on his knees and stared down at the stone floor. 'You obviously do. Since when has he had this phobia?'

'I wouldn't exactly call it a phobia but it just holds bad memories for him. It reminds him of...of the night my father died.' Vittorio's head jerked up at that but he said nothing and Lili went on, 'Last night, when Carlo came to me in the storm, I was going to ring the bell for you. I didn't know then that you weren't there. Carlo burst out crying and said he hated it because Nonna rang the bell. I didn't understand then but today I did.' Lili swallowed hard and lowered her lashes. 'Today...today he called for help for me and that...that must have taken some strength.' Lili drew in a shuddering breath. 'Stefano Bellini fled and I went to find Carlo. He was huddled under the bell, crying, sobbing that he hated it because the last time Nonno had died.'

Vittorio raked a hand through his hair and didn't speak for a long time, and when he eventually did his voice was softened by deep sorrow. 'I didn't know how deeply it had affected him. He loved Hugo very much. I suppose he associates the bell with the loss of a loved one.' He looked across at Lili. 'He must have thought he was going to lose you,' he said quietly.

The meaning of that hit Lili deep in her heart. She saw it now, the need Carlo had for her and the love. It hurt her badly because she too loved him and he was indeed going to lose her. She was going back to England tomorrow, as soon as possible. She had to go back because it hurt too much to stay.

She stood up and went to the kitchen and poured herself a glass of wine. She took it to the laundry-room door and stood gazing out into the shady courtyard. The sun was going down and soon it would be dark. She *had* to go; nothing Vittorio could say would stop her. She smiled cynically into the perfumed dusk. He hadn't tried to stop her yet and who was to say he would, ever?

She must have stood there gazing out into the courtyard for a very long time because when she finally came to her senses it was quite dark. She turned back into the kitchen, surprised that Vittorio was still there.

'What are you doing?'

'Making supper,' he told her. 'I haven't eaten for hours and nor have you——'

'What about Carlo? Are you going to leave that poor——?'

'Carlo isn't——'

'"Poor in love nor means,"' Lili echoed.

'Will you stop that?' Vittorio ordered harshly. 'My son is safe and well, safer and better off than us at the moment.' He waved a vegetable knife in her direction. 'We need to sort our lives out, Lili, then we sort out Carlo's. He has Gina with him. He loves Gina, Gina loves Carlo——'

'Who is she, this Gina?' Lili asked suspiciously. 'Is she trustworthy?'

Vittorio sighed impatiently and proceeded to slice tomatoes at an alarming rate. 'Gina is married and has children of her own and is a kind and generous lady—so is her sister who is looking after Gina's family at the moment. That is the way the Italian network functions. We all help each other at times of need. Justa wonna bigga family!'

It was too serious to laugh and Lili didn't. She felt too envious and she felt guilty for that envy. She'd never experienced it before coming here to these Tuscan hills and finding the Rossis so closely wrapped up in the family that should have been hers.

'Some damned network. I always thought *family* meant something to the Italians but I've seen little of it since I've been here.' Lili started tearing at a lettuce, blinking tears from her eyes. 'I met that poor child on a flight back home after his first term at boarding-school. Seven years old and——'

He dropped the knife and spun her to face him, eyes darkly dangerous, the grip on her arms tight to stop his anger exploding. He spoke heatedly through clenched teeth. 'My son is nearly eight. He is extremely intelligent, articulate and sophisticated beyond his years. Britain gives the finest education in the world. I want the best for my son, the very best. I'm not tearing him away from family because he hasn't got any. No brothers or sisters, no mother, no grandparents. There is *no* Rossi family. I'm all he's got and God knows I'm doing my best. Can't you understand that? Can't you see that?'

Lili's tears overflowed as she gazed up at him. They spilled and ran hotly down her cheeks. His grip lessened and she shrank away from him. Her tongue snaked out to moisten her dry lips and smooth the way for words that were torn from her heart.

'Yes, Vittorio,' she croaked rawly. 'I see it, I understand it, because ... because I've *lived* it!'

His arms dropped to his sides and Lili was free enough to walk away from him. She went to her bedroom, closing the door quietly behind her, biting back her sobs as she did it. This wasn't a time for slamming doors, or screaming, 'Poor me.' Yes, she'd lived it. She knew exactly what it was like to grow up without family and until now she was quite proud of herself for turning out so well adjusted. But now she was hurting. She wanted to feel part of someone's life, instead of ever an outsider. Her father might have loved her but he hadn't been there. Her mother had always been bound up in bitterness though she had cared for her well enough, when she'd been around. Now, wasn't it just her luck to fall in love with a man who wasn't free to love her in return and give her the security of a family?

'Coffee?'

Lili looked up, surprised she hadn't heard him enter the room, but self-pity did that sometimes— blocked off the world, she thought with cynicism. She lit the candle by the bed though it was hardly necessary—the room was bright with moonlight. She sat back against the carved wood headboard and took the coffee he offered.

'Thank you,' she murmured.

'And thank you for bringing me down to earth with a jolt,' he said quietly. 'I forget sometimes that

you too have had your share of sadness and loneli-
ness——'

'I'm not a sympathy-seeker.'

'I didn't say you were.' He sat down on the edge
of the bed. 'You've coped remarkably well——'

'And don't patronise me!'

He sighed deeply. 'Can I do no right by you?'

'Yes, get off my feet.'

He shifted an inch away from her and sipped at
his coffee. 'Now can we talk about Bellini?'

'Why?' Lili pouted. 'So you can have the full
facts before you decide whether to "deal" with him
or not?'

'I have enough on him to do what the partisans
did to Mussolini,' he stated grimly. 'He assaulted
you and frightened my child, that is enough, but I
would just like to know what provoked the attack.'

'Provoked!' Lili exclaimed in astonishment.
'That sounds as if *I* provoked *him*! As if it were all
my fault!'

Vittorio stayed calm. 'Look, Lili, if you are going
to misinterpret every word I say I'll leave now, because I am not going to be provoked any further.
You are childish and petulant, but I know you are
hurting inside and I want to help.'

'How? By talking it through and trying to do for
me what my father did for you?'

Vittorio let out a gasp of exasperation. 'Can't we
have a conversation without bringing in your father,
Carlo, Christina and half the population of
Tuscany?'

He was right, of course, but she wasn't going to
say it. 'If you must know, Bellini turned funny when

he found out that you had been here all
night——'

'What business is that of his and why did you
feel the need to tell him such a thing?'

'I didn't! I don't flash my love-life to all and
sundry, but Carlo was here and...and, well, Bellini
just jumped to that conclusion.' She didn't want to
say that Carlo, in his innocence, had once again
put his foot in it. 'He thought you were the reason
I was refusing to sell——'

'Refusing to sell——'

'Yes, refusing to sell,' Lili bit out savagely, 'and
don't you get the idea you're the reason as well.'

'Aren't I?' he husked so softly that the words
spun softly around the room like dislodged
cobwebs.

Where was resolve and sterling hearts now? She
felt his warmth so close to her feet and could reach
out and draw it to her heart—if she wanted to. And
she did want to; she wanted to hold him and say
she loved him and wanted to be in his heart...but
it was already occupied, standing room only!

'Let's make love,' Vittorio suggested temptingly,
reaching out and clasping her foot in his hand. He
caressed the arch of her foot and Lili drew on her
inner lip to stop a small cry from slipping out. 'Then
I will know if I am the reason you won't sell,' he
added with a small smile.

How easy to succumb, to let that happen, to let
him love her, but she couldn't pay the price with
pain. She just wasn't strong enough.

'You *are* one of the reasons,' she murmured, 'because of your connections with my father——'

'Please, not your father again. What about us, you and me, Lili and Vittorio, not Hugo and Emilia?'

'This isn't about us,' Lili told him levelly. 'We were talking about Stefano Bellini.' She pulled her foot away from his and he didn't try to stop her. 'I told him I wasn't going to sell, that I couldn't sell anyway because the land was yours. He said that wasn't true, that he had the deeds. He implied you were a liar——'

'He was right,' Vittorio informed her quietly.

The candle flickered in a sudden warm breeze from the window. That same breeze hushed around the back of Lili's neck.

'You lied to me?' she gasped in astonishment.

He half smiled. 'Yes, I lied to you. It's permissible to lie if it is necessary.'

'By whose moral code?'

'My very own.'

'But why, why was it necessary to lie to me?'

He looked at her as if she should know that. 'Because I was afraid I was going to lose you. I was afraid that you would just take Bellini's offer and walk out of my life. I didn't want that to happen. I'd waited too long for you to let you slip away so easily.'

Lili stared at him with hazel eyes that had taken the gold from the sun these past days but now were darkened with love and hope. But could she believe him now? Her heart was no help to make the decision; it simply stepped up the pulse and made her feel light-headed.

'It's wicked to tell lies,' she told him as Vittorio edged to her. He took her shoulders and gently urged her to him—and she went, hesitant at first, because how could you ever trust a self-confessed liar? But hearts were weak when the liar in question was the man you loved.

'Then I am wicked.' His mouth teased hers, tempting her with his devilish wickedness. His hands too tempted her with their soft, erotic pressure, cupping her breast and smoothing his intention across her senses.

But all was not entirely weak in Lili's heart. She loved this man so much that there was enough to hold a little back. A small part she held secure in bondage, restrained by the emotional chains of insecurity. She gave her body, though, and a part of her treacherous heart, because they were as wicked as his lies. For the time being that was permissible because it was necessary.

CHAPTER NINE

LILI didn't think perfection could be surpassed. But Vittorio's lovemaking was beyond the bounds of perfection this time. He was erotic and yet loving, passionate and yet controlled, gentle and yet cruel. He held back from her, teased her, had her crying out his name in frustration, but he never humiliated her. Lili tried to match him, tried to give more than she received, but in that way he was an insatiable lover.

And yet, exquisite as it all was, it was a punishment that Vittorio was unaware of. Lili loved too much and it hurt. The section of her heart she thought was on ice vaporised into puffs of white heat that had her crying and sobbing inside. She wanted all of this man, not just his beautiful sexuality. She wanted the heart that pounded so desperately against hers, as desperately as the thrusts within her.

Her emotions were in pained conflict till hedonism won. Amazingly Vittorio slowed the pace as their climax approached. His mouth was softer and his caresses lighter and all the more sensual for it. The exultation when it came was borne on a wave of love and tenderness, carried intently but not thrown away carelessly in a paroxysm of turmoil.

'Unbelievable,' he breathed through clenched teeth as with scarcely a movement they clung together, their bodies locked and slowly pulsing liquid fire through their moist bodies. There was stunning pleasure, deep, deep heart-stopping intensity of feeling, so powerful that neither could speak or move. And then wave after wave of aftershock waves that made them tremble and shudder against each other till eventually they melted exhaustedly in each other's arms.

Later, much later, Lili tried to wake Vittorio with small kisses on the side of his face but it was impossible. He'd been through so much lately, and she stopped the light kisses and let him rest. She should have been happy that he slept so contentedly, even thrilled that she had put him in that state, but she wasn't. She was restless and not really knowing why. She should be love-sated like him, in a drunken, love-overloaded coma of exhaustion, but she wasn't. Her mind kicked for attention, so hard that it gave her a headache.

Slowly, inching her body away from his, she rolled out of bed, pulled on her robe and went downstairs.

She made coffee and sat outside in the courtyard, unwinding her aching body in the clinging heat of the night. She had to make a decision about tomorrow and it was going to be difficult. An hour later she still hadn't made up her mind whether to return home to England or stay and live in her father's house till ... till when? Till Vittorio Rossi asked her to become his second wife? If.

He cared for her—he couldn't make love like that and not—but you couldn't base a life together on just that, and the lies didn't help her to come any closer to a decision. He had admitted that he had lied about the land to keep her here, and because that was a plus for her she accepted it. But the lie about him not loving his wife she couldn't accept, because she knew the truth, and that was a definite minus for her.

'So you loved your wife,' she breathed into the warm air, 'but that wife isn't here any more. I am, but am I enough for you?'

In that moment of insanity, talking to herself in the moonlight, Lili knew she wasn't. They both wanted what Hugo and Emilia had had and that was a love that was total, the very best. Lili now knew what it felt like, but sadly Vittorio didn't. Lili gazed up at the bright stars in the midnight-blue sky. A love like that was akin to possessing the stars, so close but just out of reach.

Lili went back to bed as undecisive as when she had left it.

When she awoke the next morning she knew instinctively that he wasn't lying next to her. She rolled across the bed to make sure and then buried her face in his pillow. She didn't want there to be a world when she came up for air.

'Coffee,' Vittorio murmured over her and she opened her eyes and gazed up at him. He was freshly showered, handsome and relaxed and...and, yes, happy. And why shouldn't he be? He hadn't been up half the night trying to make impossible decisions. 'I told Gina I would pick her and Carlo up at nine. It's eight now and I thought I'd drop in with Carlo on the way so he can reassure himself that you're OK.'

'No!' Confused, Lili struggled to sit up. She swept her bed-tousled hair from her face, feverishly trying to think of an excuse to put him off. Oh, no, she didn't want little Carlo here. She just wanted to go, without any painful goodbyes. Cowardly, yes, painful, yes, but facing Vittorio's son and actually *telling* him she was returning to England was far, far worse. So the decision was made—she was going, and she felt desperate about it. 'I mean . . .'

'What do you mean, sleepy-head?' Smiling, he put the coffee on the bedside table and sat down on the bed next to her. *Nice* she didn't need now.

Lili reached for the coffee, scarcely able to look at him. She hadn't the courage to tell him to his face that she was leaving because it was too painful to stay. 'I don't know what I mean,' she mumbled into her cup. 'I'm not fully awake yet.' She gulped down the hot coffee and it didn't help. Nothing would help.

'Gina is having Carlo for a few days at her home and I thought we'd have some time together.'

'I'm going home, Vittorio,' Lili blurted. It came out hotly and out of control and hit Vittorio much the same way. His eyes narrowed and his face darkened dramatically. Lili saw it for a split-second and then lowered her eyes to glare ferociously into her coffee-cup. What did he expect? Just what did he expect?

There was a long, long silence that made her feel so wretched that she wanted to fill it with a retraction.

'Yes, I know,' he said at last as if he had thought deeply on it and come to the conclusion that she was right.

Lili glanced up at him then. The darkness had gone from his face and so had the fire in his eyes. What she saw now was something far more disturbing: understanding.

'I realise you have to make certain arrangements——'

'No, Vittorio,' Lili rasped firmly. She couldn't
let him believe that she was coming back. 'There
are no "certain arrangements". I have a job at home
and a flat and a life a million miles away from these
Tuscan hills. I'm going home and I have no plans
to return in the future.' How could she deliver those
words so coldly and finally when her heart was in
such agony?

Her spoken intention sank in, then Vittorio licked
dry lips and said roughly, 'Your life is here with me
and Carlo and the memories of your——'

'No! No! No!' Lili cried, kicking her way out of
the thin cotton sheet. She grasped for her robe. 'You
don't understand, you just don't understand. I can't
live like this——'

Slowly Vittorio rose to his feet and faced her. 'I
think I've heard those very words before,' he said
heavily. 'Are you English all the same?'

Her heart stopped and fluttered and started
again. The comparison with his first wife hurt more
deeply than anything before in her life.

'No. No, we're not!' Lili protested. 'But . . . but
my reasons for wanting to leave are oceans apart
from hers.'

'I know hers—they were bleated and whined
enough times—but what are yours?'

His eyes, so dark and soft, were deeply appealing for the answer. But how could she tell him
the difference—that her love for him was so strong
that she just had to go or risk her sanity?

'I . . . I don't want Milan and the glitz,' she told
him with contempt. 'I put my demands higher than
that.' It was an insult to his wife and one he recognised. His eyes darkened so threateningly that
it powered all her hurt and pain into an outburst

that she knew would end it all. Damn him for still being affected by that woman. 'Who wants to live among the grapevines, buy their water from a tanker, pound their washing on a stone? I'm sick of all that, Vittorio Rossi, and I'll tell you something else. I'm tired of having Hugo and Emilia rammed down my throat every two minutes. This life might have been diddly dee for them but it isn't *la dolce vita* for me.'

'I was a fool to believe it could be,' he seethed quietly, his mood sinking to a depth she hadn't seen him in before. He stood in front of her, coldly unemotional. 'You are just the same, though you deny it. When are you going?' he asked.

It was a question that shook her, a cool question of acceptance that she was leaving his life. But what else could she expect? Yes, the Romans were more concerned with their practicalities than their spiritual needs.

'When I'm ready,' Lili told him unemotionally, though her fists were clenched tightly in the folds of her robe. She was beyond care now, suffering so badly that it couldn't get worse. 'Probably later this afternoon,' she added flippantly.

'Then,' he drawled, 'there is time enough for me to bring Carlo to say goodbye.'

He held her eyes as he delivered that punishing statement. And punishing it was, just when she was thinking that her suffering couldn't get worse. No, she wanted to plead, not that, not Carlo.

'I . . . I . . .' No words would come. She was suffering so deeply that the power of speech had been snatched from her.

'I . . . I what?' he urged flintily, and in that moment Lili couldn't believe his insensitivity. Was

it really his intention to hurt her so, and didn't he
know it would hurt his own son as much as her?

Something deep inside her rallied. 'I shall be very
busy today,' she said frostily. 'Far too busy for an
inquisitive child getting under my feet.' Where was
the strength coming from, she wondered, and the
cruelty to match his? 'Say goodbye to him for me,'
she added, so unemotionally that it brought a flush
of dark anger to his throat. His anger-pulse at his
jawline throbbed threateningly and Lili turned away
to pick up her coffee-cup, desperately trying to
control the shaking of her hand.

She walked to the door and felt his eyes burning
on her back, and, even knowing that this was
probably how his last wife had exited from his life,
she walked away nevertheless.

Lili cleaned the house from top to bottom after he'd
left without a word. But scrubbing and polishing
didn't help alleviate the despair. She was dreading
him coming back with Carlo, and he would though
she had told him not to. Vittorio Rossi wanted revenge and he was going to get it. She had never
suffered this depth of despair before.

She heard the car as she deliberated about
packing now or later, that deliberation taxing her
brain till it throbbed.

'Carlo?' she uttered in surprise as the boy dashed
into the house—alone.

Lili heard the car reversing and there was such
confusion in her mind that she couldn't think
straight. Surely Vittorio wouldn't go this far? Oh,
this was worse, having to tell Carlo on her own.

'Lili, Papà said as soon as the kittens are big
enough we can move them up to the house. Are

they big enough yet?' He didn't wait for an answer. 'I'll go and see.'

He sped through the kitchen, his small trainers squeaking on the newly polished tiles. Lili didn't follow, not immediately; she had to let that sink in. Vittorio must have told him that she was going and there would be no one to look after the cats . . . and . . . Carlo didn't seem at all put out. Lili didn't know whether to laugh or cry. Yes, the boy was resilient, already making plans to take over the care of the cats when she left.

'They are far too small yet,' Lili told him, squatting down next to him beside the box. The mother tabby must have gone off hunting for the kittens were alone, curled up against each other and sleeping peacefully. 'You'll have to come down every day to feed them till they are big enough.'

'Yes, I'll do that,' Carlo promised.

Suddenly Lili was weary. She was relieved that Carlo was taking it so well but despondency was depressing her further. She had overestimated so much—this child's feelings for her, even for a time Vittorio's. Both of them were taking her departure so well that they couldn't have cared much in the first place. It hurt so badly that it exhausted her.

'I'll get you a drink, Carlo,' she uttered weakly and stood up. 'Where's your father gone?'

'He's taken Gina home and then he has to meet some workers in the village and then he is coming back to take me down to Gina's. I'm staying with them for a few days. Papà said I must.'

So he'd dumped Carlo on her doorstep in between times, and it wasn't hard to understand why. He didn't want to see her ever again but he'd have the last hurtful stab by playing on her conscience with his son. But his revenge had backfired—the boy wasn't at all put out—and that made it easier for Lili to cope with. Except she wasn't coping. She turned away from Carlo and the kittens with huge tears filling her eyes.

Carlo followed her into the kitchen, racing her to the fridge for milk for the cats.

'I'll put some milk down for the cats,' he enthused, 'and then Papà said I must help you pack. I'm looking forward to that.' He balanced the carton of milk in a bowl and hurried outside again.

Deep sobs racked through Lili as she grasped at the fridge door for support. How could he do that? How could Vittorio Rossi be so heartless? Carlo helping her pack? It was unthinkable. Of course it was unthinkable! Vittorio was hoping she wouldn't have the strength to go through with it. Hope flared in her heart. He didn't want her to go; he couldn't tell her himself so had sent Carlo as his special envoy...

Wrong; if he truly cared for her his Tuscan pride wouldn't permit him to pass the buck. He'd fight for her himself. The thought hurt and so did the fact that Carlo was looking forward to helping her pack. He didn't care either and that piled on more suffering.

Nervously Lili poured Carlo a drink and when he came dashing back into the kitchen she handed it to him and said, 'You don't have to help me with the packing, Carlo. I didn't bring much anyway.'

Carlo looked disappointed. 'But Papà said you had piles. There is all Nonno's books and Nonna's pictures and her ornaments——'

'I can't take all that with me!' Lili cried, feverishly raking her hair from her fevered forehead. She didn't needed this added stress and she wished Carlo wouldn't keep referring to her father and his mistress as his grandfather and grandmother. It irritated her—they weren't, and Vittorio shouldn't go on letting Carlo believe they were. Oh, she wished Vittorio were here now; she was wound up enough to face him and do battle.

'But Papà said you would want it all——'

'Not in my holdall!' Lili cried impatiently, wishing yet again that Vittorio was here, now, so she could wring his neck for this.

Carlo began to giggle. 'I *know* you can't get it all in your holdall. The lorry will take it up.'

'The lorry? Take it up?' Lili croaked; suddenly her eyes were as wide as Carlo's. 'Take it up where?' Her voice broke on that because surely this wasn't happening?

'To our home, of course,' Carlo blurted, still giggling. 'We're all ready for you. Gina worked so hard last night to get the house...'

There was such a rushing in Lili's ears that she heard no more, but then Carlo turned and spun on his heels and belted across the room. 'Papà is back.'

The rushing in her ears stopped and she heard a car door slam. Lili didn't move; shock waves were still pounding down her spine.

Vittorio and Carlo strolled back into the house, both grinning. Lili watched, stupefied, numbed to the spot.

'Carlo says you haven't made much progress with the packing...' His eyes locked into hers but Lili immediately unlocked them. She nearly choked on a sob and went to rush across the room to the stairs.

'Never mind,' Vittorio grated, catching her wrist as she went to swing past him. 'I'm here now and

I'll help you.' He spun her so ferociously that she ended up in his arms, her heart beating so wildly that it nearly burst.

His mouth grazed lovingly against hers and in the far, far distance she heard a squeal from Carlo. You devil, Vittorio Rossi, she seethed inside, so shaken that she had lost the strength to motivate her fists.

Vittorio didn't slacken the hold he had on her, though to Carlo's eyes, Lili guessed, it would look like a fond embrace. She could never forgive him for this, never!

Suddenly a homely, dark-haired young woman walked through the open door and Carlo went to her and slipped his hand in hers and spoke excitedly to her in Italian. Vittorio tightened his grip on Lili, daring her to move.

The woman laughed and raised her hands at the sight of Vittorio and Lili and gabbled quickly in very loud Italian.

Vittorio laughed too and said in English, 'Yes, she will make a very beautiful wife for me, Gina. *Grazie*. Carlo, you can go back with Gina now. It's quite obvious you are totally incompetent as a packer so your services are no longer required. Dismissed, boy.'

With a grin Carlo rushed to his father and hugged him and then hugged Lili, and if his arms had been a few inches longer he could have encompassed the two of them, they were so tightly locked together.

Lili waited patiently till Gina and Carlo had left, though her heart was screaming for revenge. She waited till the car had started, then she tore herself from his arms.

Vittorio caught her clenched fists as they were about to pound his chest. He twisted her wrist as he grinned at her fury-reddened face.

'The custom for Italian wives to beat their husbands is rapidly fading in Tuscany, so don't do that again, *cara*.'

'No, I won't, *caro*!' Lili blazed, eyes wild and furious. 'Because I won't be here and I won't marry you—not ever, not never, just never!'

'You will, and soon——'

She was free; suddenly some strength came from somewhere and her wrist was free. She stood trembling in front of him. 'How dare you? How dare you use Carlo, and that Gina? How dare you use them against me? Have you no feelings——?'

'That's the trouble; I have too many feelings for you——'

'You have none! You're wicked and...and beastly; I can take it—but what you're doing to your son is...is unbelievable...'

'And what am I doing to my son?'

'You made him believe I was staying——'

'And you are,' he interrupted with a grin. His hands gripped her shoulders to still the fury that rattled through her. 'You are going nowhere but to my home. To be with me and Carlo——'

'No way!' Lili shook her head feverishly from side to side. She had so longed to be wanted, but now... 'All...all you want is someone to drudge for you and...and to look after your son and...and someone to heat your bed when you feel the need.'

'I can have all that without giving my heart, Lili Mayer, but that is not what I want you for. I want a wife——'

'Oh, no, but that's worse,' she cried hysterically. 'You're chasing a dream, Vittorio, and I'm not that dream. I'm not that wife you loved so much and I never can be.'

His hands tensed on her shoulders and then dropped loosely to his sides. From the corner of her eye she saw his fists ball and go white. His eyes narrowed and his lips tightened. 'I don't want a dream. I want you. It's you I love, not some damned dream. You're verging on hysteria, Lili, very nearly over the edge!'

She was; she'd just heard him say he loved her, and that couldn't be so. 'I'm...I'm not hysterical,' she breathed quickly. 'But...but I hate to be cheated, hate to be lied to. You told me a lie, Vittorio.'

His eyes widened now as if he was in doubt of her sanity. 'I thought you accepted that—that I lied about the land to keep you here.'

'I'm not talking about *that* lie——'

His look was one of complete disbelief now. 'Oh, that one is acceptable, is it? That one stroked your ego so it's OK?'

Lili nearly choked. He was right. A lie was a lie. Her head was spinning dizzily but she had to stay sane. She bit her lip as a corrected child might and tried to keep cool.

He was cool enough now when he spoke. 'So what is the other lie, Lili, or is it lies? Tell me and perhaps my explanations might appeal even more than the first.'

'There is no need to be so stuffingly sarcastic!'

'Oh, but there is, because you are playing the typical female game of tag and I'm not chasing. I love you, but it isn't enough. What more do you want?'

She stared at him. It should be enough but it wasn't. She was no better than his first wife. Her lashes flickered uncertainly. 'I . . . I want the truth,' she whispered.

'About what?' he grated.

She turned away from him then because she couldn't face it and it was all so silly because he had given her something to build on and she couldn't accept it. He loved her, and hadn't he said something about a wife? And he had sent Carlo to help her pack, to take her up to his home to live with him and his son . . . but she would have to live with him and his memories too.

Vittorio's hands were gentle as he turned her back to face him and his voice was gentle too. His touch was a sad panacea that brought a well of tears to the backs of her eyes.

'Lili, if we are going to make a life together there must be no secrets between us——'

'But there will always be lies, Vittorio,' she bleated. She raised her tear-filled eyes to his. 'I . . . I can't live with your past, you see. You lied when you told me about your wife—that she had killed your love for her with her discontent. That love didn't die. It lives on——'

'No, Lili, it doesn't live on,' he insisted. 'She destroyed our marriage, tried to destroy me with denying I was the father of our son. It's not love I have left for her but a bitterness that she should have died that way and left me to live with my guilt for not being able to make her happy.'

In despair Lili shook her head, so unsure of everything that she didn't know what to believe. 'No, you lied to me then and you are lying to me now——'

His hands tightened and his eyes narrowed. 'It is *not* a lie!'

'So your son is the liar, then?' she whispered tentatively, holding his eyes with her own, which were wide and appealing, wanting to believe and yet not wanting it. Confusion spurred more words, this time heated with emotion. 'He tells lies about his father loving his mother and...and how elated they were when he was born and... and what was the rest? Oh, yes. "Papà said even if someone is dead the loving...the loving doesn't stop."' Her voice cracked on the last syllable and she felt the hot tears on her cheeks; she could do nothing to stop them but she wasn't finished yet. 'Your life is a whole lie. The Rossi family lives a lie. You have even woven a web of lies around my father and Emilia. Carlo calls them his grandparents and they aren't— they just aren't!'

Very slowly Vittorio drew her into the warmth of his arms. His breath when it came was long and ragged. 'Oh, my Lili, my darling Lili.'

'I'm...I'm not...not your darling...anything,' she sobbed against his shoulder. 'You're cruel and heartless and you lied to me.'

'No, *cara*, no, my love,' he soothed. 'I lied to my son, not you.'

Lili's pulses slowed, so thoroughly that her blood drained. In shock she drew her head back from his warm shoulder to look into his eyes. How...how could he admit to that? 'No,' she croaked in disbelief.

'Yes,' he breathed softly, 'and another lie I stand by.' He smoothed a tear from her cheek with the crook of his little finger. 'What would you have had me tell the boy about the mother he never knew? That she was a whining socialite, never happy in the Tuscan hills her husband adored, that she wept the night she gave birth to a son because she knew she would lose that son to the Rossi vineyards? She'd craved a daughter to pamper and cosset and educate in the ways of her own. She never took to him, little Carlo. She blamed me for everything she thought she lacked in her life. Was I to tell that to my son?'

Shame hit Lili as she stared, stupefied, into Vittorio's dark eyes. It seeped into her blood and gushed around her body and hurt and hurt at every pulse it bounced off. Why hadn't she seen and understood that for herself? Why hadn't she *known*?

She pulled away from him then because her shame was too much. She held her hands up to ward him off in case he thought of taking her in his arms once again.

'Don't touch me,' she pleaded. 'I just want to be left alone.'

Slowly she walked away, her steps as leaden as her heart. Oh, God, what had she done, what had she believed? He would hate her now as much as he had hated his first wife.

Lili went through the courtyard, not seeing all that mattered to her: her father's rustic table; the glorious bougainvillaea; the tabby cat and her kittens; the bell; the green, green vineyards that stretched so far and were the very essence of a man she loved and had mistrusted so badly.

Suddenly she felt his comforting arm around her shoulders as she walked through the vineyards and she spun into his arms and sobbed into his chest, clinging to him so desperately.

'Oh, Vittorio, I've been so stupid, so blind, so...' She lifted her head and her eyes swam mistily with all that she felt for this man. 'So in love with you,' she exhaled weakly.

Vittorio Rossi smiled and raised his face to the sun and closed his eyes as if offering up a prayer. 'At last,' he breathed, 'at last she's said it.' With a grin he lowered his face and looked deeply into her hazel eyes. 'Do you know that is the first time you've actually said that you love me?'

Lili's eyes filled with more tears. 'You should have known,' she breathed softly. 'I told you with my body and the beat of my heart. I didn't speak the words but you must have known.'

He laughed. 'I thought I did that first time. I had never felt so complete and I thought you felt it too, that we belonged together, and then when I awoke you were gone from the bed. There was so much I wanted to say to you and you just weren't there.'

'And you felt dismissed when you found me doing the housework.' Lili laughed lightly. 'I was so...so embarrassed after. I loved you and wanted you and was so afraid you would think it was...just a one-time thing. I closed up because I didn't want to be hurt.'

'And I closed up too, and what a couple of idiots we were. But not any more unless you can call love and marriage idiotic.' His mouth came down to hers then and it was answer enough to quash the doubts from her mind. He did love her and she felt it in the supple pressure of his mouth, the beat of his heart against her own and the heat of his body raising her own temperature.

When their lips parted at last Lili breathed, 'But you *did* know I loved you, didn't you?' She needed to know it all—his doubts and fears, to be reassured that he really, really loved her. 'It was why you sent Carlo to help me pack, and why you were so cruel and such a liar and . . . and so tricky. But, Vittorio, how did you know when I'd never spoken the words?' She bit her lip in shame. He had said the words and she hadn't believed them and she had said nothing. 'How did you know I loved you so very much?'

Vittorio's eyes deepened with the love she could read so clearly now. 'I knew, my darling Lili, because it was meant to be.'

'A love made in heaven?' she teased, her eyes bright with mischief.

Vittorio grew serious, his eyes darkening. 'No, not made in heaven,' he told her gently, 'but here on earth, by two people who loved us very much.'

Lili tilted her head and gazed at him quizzically. His arms were still around her and his hands smoothed down her back in small reassuring caresses. There was warmth all around them, the buzz of bees, the sweet scent of grapes ripening on the vine.

'Your father was one of them, Lili. He wanted you here, to show you all that he had learnt, to love as he had loved.'

'And I didn't fail him, Vittorio. I never want to leave here. It was the most precious gift he could ever leave me—you. But, Vittorio, you said *two* people who loved us very much?'

Suddenly Lili felt a whisper of air on the back
of her neck and she had a strange feeling that she
and Vittorio were not alone in the hot vineyards.
It was a safe feeling, warm and comforting and not
at all frightening. She waited for his answer.

'Emilia,' he said at last.

'Emilia?'

'Yes, *amore*, Emilia. You said I deceived Carlo
into thinking she and Hugo were his grandparents;
well——'

Lili let out a very small gasp, a mixture of anticipation and pleasure. Suddenly she knew; before
he said it she knew! 'Go on,' she breathed huskily.

'They were,' he said hesitantly. 'Hugo not by
blood but . . . but by marriage. Emilia *was* his grandmother——'

'And. . .and your mother,' Lili whispered happily,
her eyes shining with all that that meant to her. She
should have known; she should have worked it all
out and known. Vittorio's love for the old villa, his
love for Hugo. And her father knew that Vittorio
would look after his mother if anything happened
to him—that was why he'd left the house to his
daughter. His legacy of love for the lost years.

Vittorio nodded and brought a hand up to
smooth away a wisp of tawny hair that a breath of
wind had fluffed across her forehead.

'You sound happy about that,' he murmured.

'Oh, I am,' she smiled. 'I really am. But, Vittorio,
you said not by blood but by marriage. Does that
mean that my father and your mother *were*
married?'

'Not for a long time,' Vittorio told her. 'Your
father was divorced and the village priest not sym-
pathetic and it didn't seem to matter for a while,

but then your father wanted to make it right. They eventually married in France where your father had lived.'

Lili sighed deeply and contentedly. 'Oh, Vittorio, I'm so glad about that. It makes it all complete and it makes me feel as if at last I've come home. It also answers so many things about you and this place and why you didn't want me to sell it.' Her smile faded but she wasn't unhappy. 'Oh, Vittorio. You could have told me that Emilia was your mother the first day I arrived but you didn't want me to be swayed by such sentimentality, did you?'

'I thought you had enough to cope with coming to terms with your own father's life here. Telling you about Emilia would have complicated your emotions even more. I wanted you to come to your own decision, to love this place as your father and Emilia did, to find what they had found.'

'And I did find it but couldn't accept it because I felt so insecure.' She sighed. 'Like you and Carlo, I had no family. I don't think I ever realised just how lonely I was till I fell in love with you. I was jealous of your first wife, jealous of your closeness with my father, and when I found a picture of Emilia I even felt a stab of jealousy over her too. I wanted what they had so very much.'

Vittorio tightened his arms around her. 'And it's what I've always wanted too and the moment you arrived and stepped out of that dusty Fiat I knew I could have it.'

'Oh, Vittorio,' Lili laughed. 'Another lie?'

'Sort of,' he grinned, swooping down to kiss her fully on the lips, not a lingering kiss, though. 'I told you, I didn't like you before you arrived but when you did I could see trouble ahead. It was just like your father to leave us each other and sit back and watch the fireworks.'

Lili laughed. One day she would tell Vittorio about that strange breath of air on the back of her neck. For now she was happy to slip her arms around *his* neck.

'And now that the fireworks are over,' she husked mischievously. 'What plans have you for us?'

'Immediately or somewhere in the future?'

She felt the firmness of his body against hers. 'I *know* your immediate plans but what of to-morrow? Are we to make our home in the Villa Libra?'

He threw his dark head back and laughed. 'What? No running water, no electricity——'

'You hypocrite!' Lili cried on a laugh. 'So much for the values of life!'

'Well, *cara*, when our marriage runs into diffi-culties we will come down here and remind our-selves of them——'

'Difficulties!' Lili exploded. 'You are already anticipating some, are you?' With mock indig-nation she pushed at his chest and turned and ran, gathering her skirt around her to speed her through the crowded vines.

'Plenty,' she heard him growl behind her and then she was falling . . . laughing and falling.

Vittorio pinned her to the ground in the shade of the vine. His mouth was warm and persuasive on hers, his hands seductive as they pushed her skirt aside to caress her sun-bronzed thighs. The kiss was everything: the sun, the life, the very best. Then he drew back from her to look down into her beauti-ful face.

'Later,' he husked, 'much later, how would you like a long, cool swim in the pool?'

Lili groaned.

'Then relax in the poolside jacuzzi?'

Lili's eyes widened.

'And then I'll cook you a beautiful steak on my halogen hob.'

Lili moaned with hunger.

'Then I'll put you to bed between silk sheets.'

Lili smiled softly. 'You have all that and yet once you said it meant nothing.'

'It is nothing without a love like this,' he said with deep passion.

And Lili understood when his mouth came to hers and burned with such raw excitement. Nothing mattered but the love between them; nothing mattered in the whole wide world but this total love.

Suddenly she covered his hand as it came to caress her waiting breast. 'Vittorio?' she murmured in a small voice. 'Just one thing; it's not really important—no, not at all really—but well . . . you do have a washing-machine, don't you?'

He didn't answer, not one word. His kiss was no answer either, nor his hands as they enfolded her into his love and desire, nor his body as it melded heatedly against hers.

Lili let out a small gasp of desire and need. Perhaps at a time like this it was a silly question. Yes, a very silly question, but nevertheless . . .

Mills Boon

Proudly present
to you...

BETTY NEELS' 100ᵀᴴ ROMANCE

Betty has been writing for Mills & Boon Romances for over 20 years. She began once she had retired from her job as a Ward Sister. She is married to a Dutchman and spent many years in Holland. Both her experiences as a nurse and her knowledge and love of Holland feature in many of her novels.

Her latest romance *'AT ODDS WITH LOVE'* is available from August 1993, price £1.80.

Next Month's Romances

Each month you can choose from a wide variety of romance with Mills & Boon. Below are the new titles to look out for next month, why not ask either Mills & Boon Reader Service or your Newsagent to reserve you a copy of the titles you want to buy – just tick the titles you would like and either post to Reader Service or take it to any Newsagent and ask them to order your books.

Please save me the following titles:	Please tick	√
SIMPLY IRRESISTIBLE	Miranda Lee	
HUNTER'S MOON	Carole Mortimer	
AT ODDS WITH LOVE	Betty Neels	
A DANGEROUS MAGIC	Patricia Wilson	
TOWER OF SHADOWS	Sara Craven	
THE UNMARRIED BRIDE	Emma Goldrick	
SWEET BETRAYAL	Helen Brooks	
COUNTERFEIT LOVE	Stephanie Howard	
A TEMPORARY AFFAIR	Kate Proctor	
SHADES OF SIN	Sara Wood	
RUTHLESS STRANGER	Margaret Mayo	
BITTERSWEET LOVE	Cathy Williams	
CAPTIVE BRIDE	Rosemary Carter	
WILLING OR NOT	Liza Hadley	
MASTER OF NAMANGILLA	Mons Daveson	
LOVE YOUR ENEMY	Ellen James	
A FOOLISH HEART	Laura Martin	

If you would like to order these books in addition to your regular subscription from Mills & Boon Reader Service please send £1.80 per title to: Mills & Boon Reader Service, Freepost, P.O. Box 236, Croydon, Surrey, CR9 9EL, quote your Subscriber No:................................. (If applicable) and complete the name and address details below. Alternatively, these books are available from many local Newsagents including W.H.Smith, J.Menzies, Martins and other paperback stockists from 13 August 1993.

Name:...

Address:...

....Post Code:........................

To Retailer: If you would like to stock M&B books please contact your regular book/magazine wholesaler for details.

You may be mailed with offers from other reputable companies as a result of this application. If you would rather not take advantage of these opportunities please tick box ☐